TAINTED REALITY

IN THE WRONG HANDS, THE CURE
BECAME FATAL

ASHLEY FONTAINNE

OTHER BOOKS BY ASHLEY FONTAINNE

The Magnolia Series (written with Lillian Hansen):
Blood Ties
Blood Loss
Blood Stain

Mystery/suspense novels:
Fatal Agreements
Suicide Lake
Empty Shell
Night Court
Whispered Pain
Number Seventy-Five

Eviscerating the Snake Trilogy:
Accountable to None
Zero Balance
Adjusting Journal Entries

Paranormal/suspense:
Growl
The Lie
Operation Jade Helmet

Poetry and Short Stories:
Ruined Wings
Fine as Frog Hair
Ramblings of a Mad Southern Woman

TAINTED REALITY

IN THE WRONG HANDS, THE CURE
BECAME FATAL

ASHLEY FONTAINNE

PRAISE FOR ASHLEY FONTAINNE

"I absolutely love this woman's style and plots. Have to read anything and everything she writes. Awesome talent! Thanks, Ashley Fontainne, for creating such memorable works!"
~ *Janelle Taylor, New York Times bestselling author*

"Ashley Fontainne proves with *Number Seventy-Five* that she's a talent to watch."
~ *Raymond Benson, author of The Black Stiletto series*

"Ashley Fontainne has written her best and most compelling book to date. A multi-layered thriller with strong characters and emotions that grab the reader from page one to the shocking ending. Murder, betrayal, and lies bind a Southern family in a very *Fatal Agreement*."
~ *Elaine Raco Chase, bestselling author*

"A gritty, realistic, deftly crafted novel, *Ruined Wings* is a simply riveting read from beginning to end…a significant, relevant, and highly recommended addition for personal reading lists, as well as community and academic library collections."
~ *Midwest Book Reviews*

"Ashley Fontainne has penned a captivating story with her prime character torn between deep personal anguish and a new danger to the people he has sworn to serve and protect…This is a must read for anyone who likes getting the hell scared out of them, which is what Ashley Fontainne does best in her writings."

~Arkansas Hall of Fame writer Del Garrett, author of WHILE THE ANGELS SLEPT

"…hooked me into this story from the very first line. Tidwell is an empathetic character that readers will root for in his rise to heroism. Tidwell is reminiscent of Craig Johnson's Walt Longmire: rugged, aloof, extremely broken, and far more complicated than what he appears to be on the surface. As for the plot, fans of Frank Perretti's *This Present Darkness Series* will enjoy it. Though Fontainne's story has an obvious Christian message, I believe the story's pervasive darkness and eventual redemption can be appreciated by the secular reader as well, especially one who is into paranormal thrillers. Overall, *Many* is profoundly engaging and emotionally wrought. At times, I'd even say it is outright terrifying. Ashley Fontainne is truly a master of the description required for the short story, revealing just enough to draw the reader into the plot."

~ Timothy R. Baldwin for Readers' Favorite

Table of contents

Chapter 1 - Paralyzed

Saturday, December 20th – 10:15 a.m.

EVERETT SITS ON THE cold chair in the lab while staring at all the dusty, ruined equipment. Though he'd been to the facility twice to clean up after Daryl Riverside kidnapped him and killed the rest of the staff and test subjects, the area is still messy. Riverside had destroyed all the computers, leaving piles of crushed plastic and metal innards strewn across the room. He breathed a sigh of relief while conducting an inventory earlier, discovering the only items Daryl ruined were the computers. With no human inhabitants to care for what was left of the workspace, dust accumulated over all the shiny metal and glass surfaces.

Even though Dirk and the others had removed the bodies of Dr. Thomas and Dr. Flint, along with the twenty-five former addicts, the entire underground haven retains the rancid odor of death. The worst of the stench emanates from the lab. Dirk had been preoccupied with burying the twenty-seven innocents murdered in a secluded spot near the cave and neglected the lab. When Everett returned to the facility for the first time three months after the nightmare in Laredo, he'd been greeted by carnage. Rows and rows of cages housing hundreds of mice for testing were full of rank, rotting little corpses.

The stench faded over time yet traces of it remain embedded in every crevice of the workspace. When the small group arrived earlier and the doors were unlocked, the odor nearly made him puke.

He is exhausted; mentally and physically spent, with no reserves left to get up and find a pen or figure out what to do next. His mind is awash in a buzz of white nothingness. Everything around him is familiar yet seems out of place. Vials, beakers, syringes, cages, computers, all of it. He feels just like a prepubescent boy who spent countless hours looking through his father's stash of porn, and then actually seeing his first naked girl. The sensation of not having a clue what to do next has left him dazed and confused.

The nightmare of the fact dead people are now walking around eating the living makes him feel like he is the star of the most colossal horror movie ever conceived.

"Dr. Berning?"

Without raising his head, he sighs, long and deep. "Yes?"

Dirk walks across the room and sits on a stool on the other side of the counter. "Have you eaten or drank anything yet?"

"No."

"I figured. Here." Dirk slides over a bottle of water and a protein bar.

"I'm afraid you'd be wasting precious supplies, Dirk. I'd just throw it up. My body's reaction to the unreal chain of events won't be pretty. Old man's stomach, you know."

"If you don't eat, you'll pass out. I'm the only one here qualified to start an IV and believe me, that's not saying much. Haven't done it in years. I'm rusty, so it would be a painful experience."

Blowing out his breath, he grabs the bottle and bar, taking two small sips and one little bite. "There. Happy?"

Dirk's lips curve into a snide grin. "First thing that's made me smile all day."

He stares at Dirk's face, noting the worry and stress behind the man's dark eyes. "Huh. Guess we won't take even the smallest of things for granted anymore, right?"

"Nope." Dirk leans across the counter and picks up an empty vial, rolling it around with his fingers, studying it with mild curiosity. "Now, stop moping around and tell me what you need from me."

"And us."

Both men turn at the sound of Kevin Warton's voice. The former soldier stands in the doorway, cheeks flushed, hands clasped in front of a slender waist. The rest of the men are behind him.

"I...I don't even know where to start. All this is just too unreal to even grasp." Everett hangs his head in shame. "I'm at a loss as to what to do next. My mind is in total gridlock. Overstimulation of my neurons has rendered me useless."

"Getting the lab cleaned up and ready to use seems like a good place to start." Kevin steps inside; the others follow and in seconds, the lab is full of six men, all staring at Everett and waiting for instructions.

"Excellent idea. This place stinks." Thomas Porterfield crinkles his nose. "I hate the stench of death."

"If we don't want to keep smelling it above ground then we need to get going. We've got faith in you, Doc. None of us would have signed up for this gig if we didn't."

Kevin's comment snaps Everett out of his funk. He pulls his gaze from the dusty table and stares into the man's eyes. "Your loyalty was sorely misplaced, Mr. Warton. As I told Mr. Kincanon earlier, my contribution to mankind was to wipe out addiction. That's been accomplished but it certainly doesn't matter now. The world has been hit—no, invaded—with some sort of biological contagion never seen or heard of before. I can't fix this. We can't fix this. It's over, don't you get that?"

Thomas moves closer, bright green eyes full of anger, stopping less than five feet from Everett and glares at him. The familiar, childhood fear of a burly bully ready to pounce on him makes his heart race.

"Pull yourself together, Dr. Berning. Fall apart later after you figure out what sort of bug we're dealing with. At the very least, we need to know how it's transmitted and how to protect ourselves from getting infected."

"Thomas—please." Dirk holds up his hand, silencing Thomas's fury. "Anger isn't going to help either. Dr. Berning? I know you're upset—we all are—but we're safe here. No one knows the location and the doors are secured. No one will get in here unless we let them inside. We have plenty of food and supplies to last for a year—longer if we ration wisely. Treat this nightmare as your degree thesis. Figure out what the hell we are dealing with first and then formulate a counterattack. You'll be graded on your success."

He tries stopping the anger from seeping into his voice, but it doesn't work. He glares at Dirk. "We left those people out there and didn't even check on them. What if they survived the crash and needed our help?"

Kevin opens his mouth to reply but Dirk snaps his fingers, and the man remains silent. "Trust me, they didn't survive. They came in too fast, and no one ejected before the jet slammed into the ground."

"You can't possibly know for sure! If I recall correctly, you were on top of me plus the cloud cover blocked any visibility. What if one of them survived the initial impact? We condemned them to death without even batting an eye!"

"Dr. Berning, I realize you have no combat experience, but we all do." Dirk lowers his voice and eases his tone. "No one could have lived after crashing at such a high rate of speed. With all the shit going on, that's what you're worried about?"

"Yes!" He rises, pacing the floor like a maniac. "It took us what—less than two hours—to turn into selfish creatures? Ones unwilling to help save lives. We just walked away so we could save our own asses, and now all of you are looking to me to save the remainder of humanity. Hypocrisy at its finest. You're all government grunts for sure!"

"I don't recall seeing you turn around and run to their aid, ol' noble Dr. Berning." Thomas glares at him, cheeks flushing to deep crimson. "Nor do I remember hearing you ask any of us to render assistance. Congratulations on your newest discovery—you're just as human as the rest of us and when it comes down to brass tacks, you save your own ass first."

In a fit of rage, Everett grabs the closest beaker and launches it against the wall. "You're right, Mr. Porterfield. I'm a selfish bastard, which is why I won't do a fucking thing to solve this—but it's not because I don't want to—it's because I simply cannot."

The room falls silent after his tirade. Without looking at any of them, he storms out of the lab and limps toward his old room as terror, fury, and shame jockey for control of his mind.

By the time he reaches the door, terror takes control. He succumbs to the overwhelming fear and collapses onto the old cot, body quaking as the magnitude of the situation sweeps through his mind.

He sobs, wishing Dr. Flint and Dr. Thomas were still alive because he has no clue what to do in this strange, new reality.

Chapter 2 - Liberating the School

Saturday, December 20th – 10:15 a.m.

WALT ADDISON GLANCES in the rearview mirror just in time to see Martha's Humvee take out two of the shuffling corpses in the parking lot. Blood and gore explode over the hood and windshield as the vehicle bobs. Tires mash the bodies, pulverizing them into piles of flesh, leaving behind nothing except a mangled conglomeration of flesh and torn clothing. His stomach lurches when a small horde of the dead descend on their downed comrades.

"Interesting. At least I know they aren't picky eaters. Good information to hang on to for later."

Focusing back on the road in front of him, he guns the engine. The tires squeal after cranking the wheel to the right, turning onto Highway 270. An unmanned roadblock of several Humvees and barricades looms in the distance. Squinting, he searches for any signs of soldier, sees none, and pushes his foot down harder on the pedal, blowing through the wooden markers. Glancing in the side mirror, he sees Martha, Reed, Turner, and the others follow his lead.

While driving, thoughts of what happened during the last three hours are threatening to shove him over sanity's edge. He's prepared for a variety of catastrophic events, including a biological attack. Curt Campbell's vision of the end happened because of an electromagnetic pulse attack either from a foreign or domestic enemy. Lamar Wilson's was global warming, and his basement is full of all sorts of charts, graphs, research reports and the like, all touting the immense damage created by millions of people living on Mother Earth. During monthly prepper meetings, Lamar bent ears about environmental pollutants, dumping of toxic waste, and climate change, among other things.

Another member who was quite vocal in his opinions was Cary Woodson. His end of the world scenario revolved around some nutso dictator sitting in his office, pushing the red button, and detonating a nuclear bomb. During the last few years, Cary also voiced concerns over the likelihood of some terrorist group bringing or even manufacturing a dirty bomb on American soil.

Yet another member feared invasive species taking over. He quietly chuckles at the memory of Ronald Hope standing in front of the group with a PowerPoint presentation of the dangers of kudzu overtaking everything with their clingy vines. Ronald believed the plant would choke out the ground, thus ending the ability of farmers to grow enough food to feed an ever-growing society.

Though some reasons seemed almost comical, all the members of the prepper group agreed the world couldn't survive another fifty years. Most of them are his age, and there was an unspoken common understanding the end probably wouldn't happen during their lifetimes. However, for the sake of their families and future generations, they all agreed to be prepared.

Ever since leaving the military, he's leaned toward a biological attack because he'd seen up close and personal the effects of chemical weapons on soldiers and innocent civilians. Any madman with money could acquire access to dangerous, volatile chemicals. A man with power and connections could hire—or force—scientists to create new strains, new forms, new atrocities capable of destroying flesh by dangling money.

Yet none of their training, none of the off-the-wall scenarios came close to preparing them for what is happening now. The thought of people turning into walking corpses feasting on the flesh of others was too preposterous and laughable to even contemplate, and yet, that is exactly what they are dealing with—horror movie shit.

"Fucking government. I guarantee you they did this. In their quest to conquer the entire world, they unleashed something deadly into the populace."

Pushing the insanity aside, he forces himself to concentrate on the task at hand because there simply isn't time, and he certainly isn't the person, to figure out how the hell dead bodies reanimate.

The plan to storm the school is extremely risky, and since he is alone with his thoughts, his true feelings emerge. No matter the moral reasons behind the crazy quest, the group is heading straight into a death trap. He is a good bullshitter and could make it past the freaked-out grunts with minimal effort, but the infamous Lt. Pack—and others like him still inside the school—won't be so easy to manipulate. The best course of action would be to take Lt. Pack out of the picture.

The thought makes his head spin. As the school parking lot comes into view, he slams a fist against the dashboard. "Dammit, Turner! All over a piece of ass! We should be arriving at the cave, or at least close, by now."

Releasing a bit of anger helped calm his nerves. In seconds, he pulls into the parking lot of Malvern High School and the place is packed and not one space available. Cars, trucks, and SUVs litter the blacktop, some even parked along the small berm separating the school from the street. He zigzags through the silent vehicles until reaching the back area where the teachers and staff normally park, only to find more Humvees crammed in the spaces than when they fled earlier.

Numerous dead bodies lay on the blacktop from the earlier skirmish, so he averts his gaze, refusing to let the horror of the situation take control of his mind.

Swinging around so the vehicle is facing the exit, he shuts the engine down and waits until the remainder of the group arrives and parks in the exact same manner. Deputies Bailey and Allsop are the final stragglers. Taking a deep breath, he offers a silent prayer for God to watch over them and exits the Humvee.

Lamar walks over to the window and peers inside, scouring the interior. Walt waits until everyone else gathers close to speak. "Allsop and Bailey—since you two are still in uniform and locals will recognize you, stay stationed by the back door. Once we get groups outside, they won't hesitate to follow a friendly face. Keep your engines running and leave together once full up."

"Gotcha," both men reply in unison.

"The first item on the agenda is finding Lt. Pack, and anyone else ranked sergeant or above. Let me do the talking. I'll convince them an urgent message from the governor awaits and they need to follow us. We'll bring them out back, secure them, and then start evacuating the civilians."

"This ain't gonna work, Dad. What if—"

"No time for what ifs, Turner." Reed interrupts. "Your dad's right. We must do this now. Time's wasting. We walk in with a purpose and don't veer from it. All those people trapped inside are depending on us to get them to safety, they just don't know it yet."

"Walt, what happens if we come across someone who's sick?" Martha asks.

"Bypass them for now. We must get the healthy out first."

Lamar joins them with a smile on his face. "Don't worry, y'all. This is gonna be a piece of cake. There're twenty-five grunts inside, two sergeants, and only one dirty lieutenant."

Walt grins. "What's their position?"

"A lone grunt is stationed by the main door, and the lieutenant and other sergeant are huddled together in the kitchen staring at maps. Both look scared outta their granny panties."

"Guess there ain't no need for my little story to lure them out with then." Walt chuckles. "Easy pickings."

Reed points to the building. "How many people are inside, Lamar? Do any look sick?"

"Didn't see any that looked sick, but kinda hard to tell without a closer look. I counted about two hundred civvies, and they're all gathered near the kitchen doors. There's a slew of dead bodies close to the front entrance. Seems they're steering clear of them."

"Jesus, how in the world will we get everyone out in time?" Turner's face blanches. "And what about everyone else who ain't here? How we gonna warn them what's going on?"

"One crisis at a time, son. Okay, here's the plan: Martha, you and Turner come with me. We'll get Lt. Pack and his cohort. Lamar, you go with Reed and fetch the other fool. Deputy Bailey, you and Allsop got your cuffs with you?"

"Yes." Bailey nods. "But we each only have one set."

"Then I guess one of them will just need to take a nap." Walt pats the butt of his rifle. "After we secure the trio, we'll round up the remaining grunts and then get our friends and neighbors to safety. Got it?"

They all nod in agreement.

Walt and Martha lead the group across the blacktop toward the back door, guns ready and hearts pounding with dread.

Once in place, he glances at his beautiful wife, noting the fear behind her eyes, along with determination. Her blue eyes shimmer in the bright sunlight. He winks and motions with his head for her to move behind him. She returns the wink and complies.

Yanking the door open, he bursts inside the kitchen, gun pointed at the head of the lieutenant. Martha and Turner split off and flank right, their own weapons trained on the sergeant.

"Hands up and mouths shut, or my face is the last one you'll ever see." Walt orders.

The two men freeze. Lt. Pack stands next to the seated sergeant, his hulking frame crammed inside an ill-fitting uniform stained with blood. Two rifles sit on the counter out of reach, Beretta M9s resting snugly on both of their hips.

Sizing his quarry up, he surmises the lieutenant is six-foot-two, possesses the solid build of a linebacker, has a harsh face with a square jawline and dark brown, unreadable eyes. Lt. Pack is a formidable opponent, maybe forty, judging by the deep lines on his forehead and around his orbital bones. From his periphery, he sees the sergeant is smaller yet leaner. Maybe thirty tops.

Reed and Lamar come up from the right, moving past them until reaching the entryway to the cafeteria. He gives a slight nod and the two disappear through the doors.

The lieutenant's steely, furious gaze never leaves his own, and with slow, calculated movements, he raises his arms in compliance with Walt' order. The sergeant next to him is young, scared, and stupid, and like a fool, he reaches for his weapon. His arm moves less than two inches before Martha rams the butt of her rifle into his wimpy face, knocking the bastard from his perch.

"That wasn't necessary. He is just doing his job."

"Shut up, Lt. Pack." Walt's deep baritone commands attention. "I ain't got no time for giving orders twice. Here's a new set: help your buddy to his feet and let's take this out back. No tricks or sudden movements or we will shoot. Got it?"

The hatred behind the soldier's eyes is almost palpable. Walt grins, but it isn't a friendly gesture. Martha and Turner move to the door and open it. The lieutenant finishes giving Walt the evil eye, bends down, and yanks the sergeant to his feet. In seconds, they are back out in the bright daylight.

Allsop and Bailey are ready. They cuff both soldiers.

"Local militia. I knew it." Lt. Pack glares at his captors. "Been begging for years for the higher-ups to wipe you all out. Now, when the world crashes around us, you bastards swoop in and try to take control when you have no idea what's really going on!"

Walt's right arm connects with Pack's bulbous nose, and the force of the punch knocks the big man to his knees. "That's for not keeping your hole shut and for giving the order to kill innocent people.

Fucking pussy! You're supposed to help your fellow citizens, not kill them!"

"That's enough! We don't have time to see who has the bigger dick between the two of you." Martha stomps her feet. "Lt. Pack, are you still in communication with HQ?"

"Like I'm really going to answer that honestly." Pack spits out a mouthful of blood in Walt's direction. The heavy dollop lands next to his boot.

Martha immediately reacts, jamming the tip of the rifle against Pack's temple. "There's a bullet in here with your name on it. If you want it to remain in the barrel and not rip through your head, you'll comply."

"Fuck you, bitch."

"Hold up there, honey." Walt fears she's about to make good on her word as anger flashes behind her vibrant blue eyes and the electrical current in the air shifts. "Geez, you're just as antsy as Chief Parker. Let's see what happens with this."

He snatches the radio from Pack's waist, but before getting the chance to test his theory, Lamar and Reed return with a captive soldier who looks like he is close to pissing himself or fainting. He mentally bets a wet stain will appear on the front of the fatigues right before the government tool passes out.

"Let's get you tied up real nice so you can join your fellow killers." Lamar extracts a short length of nylon rope from his pocket and in a flash, binds the third hostage.

"What's your call sign, boy?" Walt directs the question to the soldier Martha clocked earlier.

A pair of defiant green eyes already swelling from the impact of the rifle glare at Martha, yet the boy remains silent. For emphasis, she raises her weapon above her head as though a baseball bat. "I'll give you to three, and I've already ticked off one and two."

"Don't you say a word!" Pack yells.

Shifting his gaze between the lieutenant and Martha, the boy's defiance dims, replaced by dejection. "Contain 2 Actual. Won't do you a bit of good though. Ain't nobody answering on the other end. Been silent for the past ten minutes."

Walt ignores him and presses the button. "Contain 2 Actual to base."

The sounds of static fill the back parking lot. He tried three more times, each with the same results.

"I told you. We're on our own," the sergeant mutters.

"Then there ain't nobody to miss you." Walt glances around and notices a small area to the right used to store garbage. It is surrounded by a ten-foot chain link fence to keep foraging animals out. The only way in or out is from a door outside the kitchen. Motioning toward the area, he addresses the group. "Let's get them secured in there and get to work. Got a lot of people to rescue."

"We can help. you know." Pack offers.

"Pft! You've been so helpful already." Martha grumbles.

"I'm serious. You don't really think we were going to just kill those poor people and leave, do you?"

Turner steps forward, aiming the barrel of his rifle inches from Pack's head. "Right up until the end, government puppets still lie. Move!"

Walt grins, proud of his boy for finally seeing the light, yet sad it took him so long.

Chapter 3 - Adventures at Walmart

Saturday, December 20th – 10:25 a.m.

REGINA IS SHAKING by the time she pulls into the parking lot. Squinting through the bloody windshield, she silently curses the fools who prepped the Humvee. After demolishing the first dead corpse she hit leaving the jail, brain matter and other chunks of gore stuck to the glass and when she turned flicked on the wipers, no cleaner came out because someone neglected to check the windshield washer fluid levels.

Then again, who had time to address such a minute task when people are turning into undead cannibals?

Susie cried the entire four-minute drive and no amount of comfort offered by Jesse seemed to help. Regina remained silent, using all her concentration on navigating the clogged roads full of stalled vehicles and the dead. However, the minute the familiar location appeared, the girl's tears dried up. She almost laughs at the absurdity.

Welcome to Walmart. Get in and hunker down as the world ends! That should be their new motto.

She scans the area, grateful there are only a few cars parked in the spots, yet even without all the crazy shit happening, it is sort of eerie to see the vast expanse of blacktop empty. The only other time she's seen so many available spaces was after the building suffered major damage from an F-3 tornado in 2003.

"Mom?"

"Yes?"

Jesse leans forward while peering out the window. "I think we'll need to use the back bay door in automotive."

Regina slows the Humvee down to a crawl and follows Jesse's gaze, homing in on the front glass doors. Inside the first set are countless bodies in various states of dismemberment, and a throng of at least fifteen creatures surround the pile, ripping and chomping their way through the bloody mess.

Susie screams.

"Hush, Susie!" Regina's heart skips two beats as the ghoulish diners turn their attention toward the noise.

Jesse climbs into the backseat and cradles the terrified girl in her arms, trying to quell her fears, but the gesture doesn't work because Susie continues screaming at the top of her voice, forcing Jesse to clamp her hand over the girl's mouth.

Regina tromps on the gas pedal and jerks the wheel, zigzagging through the parking lot toward the back of the store.

"Hurry, Mom! Look! Only one bay door is open!"

Seconds later, she pulls into the first bay, thankful all the other doors are shut, and no one is inside. She exits the Humvee and whispers, "Stay put."

In a few steps, she is at the bay door, grabs the latch, and pulls the rollup metal door down. A a cold shiver races up her spine at the sound of feet running and the disgusting, mewling grumbles, which grow louder. Refusing to look and see how close the horde is, she focuses all her attention on securing the bay door. The second it shuts, she steals a peek through the small, dirty window. Her mouth goes dry upon seeing the mob of dead less than twenty feet from the door.

Spinning around, she eyes all the remaining doors and though closed, they aren't locked. She sprints to each, head pounding and heart racing until all are sealed tight. While jogging back toward the Humvee, the weird mixture of Jesse cooing gibberish to Susie and the primal gurgling of the dead makes her head swim.

Yanking the passenger door open, she gently latches onto Susie's trembling arm, lowers her head, and whispers, Susie? Susie! Look at me. Stop crying, we're safe. I know this is terrifying, and believe me, I'm scared just like you, but now isn't the time to fall apart. We've got to get inside and make sure others who are just as frightened have a safe place to go. Okay?"

Susie clamps her eyes shut while her frail body trembles. Regina feels the tension in her muscles and the racing pulse. Susie opens her eyes at the same time as her mouth, gulping in a huge intake of air.

Regina knows what is coming next. She's witnessed panic attacks happen to Jesse hundreds of times throughout the years. Over the din of the clanging, grunting monsters pounding on the metal doors, and the fear of any inside the building within hearing distance, she has no choice. She balls up her fist and clocks Susie right under the chin, knocking her unconscious.

"Glad you never did that to me when I freaked out." Jesse deadpans.

"Always the comedienne. Stay here with her until I secure the waiting area inside."

Jesse's eyes are wide and full of fear; pale cheeks tinged in red. She nods once and moves closer to Susie's limp body, adjusting her head to a comfortable position against the backrest.

Retrieving the rifle from the passenger seat, she shuts the door, mouths *I love you; lock it* to Jesse, and pauses until hearing the telltale *click*.

Forcing herself to calm down and control her labored breathing, she ignores the burning sensation of the blood from the cut on her head skimming the edge of her eye. Blinking to refocus, she walks over to the door leading inside and peers through the glass.

Nothing but automotive equipment, an empty register, and spilled coffee in the waiting area.

Thank God!

Stepping inside, she sweeps the area, making sure nothing is hiding. The sounds from outside are muffled, but new ones catch her attention. The distinct noise of someone sobbing emanates from further inside the store. Assuming the noise is from terrified shoppers, she tunes the sound out. The obnoxious Christmas music over the loudspeaker blares, yet she homes in on the noises closest to her position, which she concludes are light breathing, and the faintest recitation of The Lord's Prayer.

Edging past the counter, she cranes her neck and peers over. Crumpled into a tight ball, back pressed against the wall leading to the automotive bay, sits a frightened, elderly woman dressed in the traditional blue vest worn by all employees, with mounds of thick, gray hair sticking up in all directions. Her face is buried in wrinkled hands.

Moving closer, Regina stops when about five feet away. "Ma'am, it's okay. Shhh, be quiet now. I'm a cop and I'm here to help."

For a few seconds, she wonders if the elderly woman heard the words, but finally, the lady raises a tear-stained face from her hands and terror switches over to relief. "Chief Parker?"

She almost gasps. "Mrs. Singleton?"

"Oh, thank the Lord above!"

She squats down while motioning for Mrs. Singleton to be quiet. "Where's the button to release the gate?"

Mrs. Singleton points to the right. Without a word, Regina rises, moves to the other side of the counter, and pushes the button. The metal gate appears from its hiding spot in the ceiling. She cringes at the noise and slowness of the descent.

Once closed, she moves closer and peeks through the slats, grateful to only see racks of shelves.

She rushed back over to Mrs. Singleton, making sure to keep her voice low. "Are you injured?"

The woman shakes her head.

"Good. Okay, I'm bringing in Jesse and another young girl. Are you up to watching over another while Jesse and I secure the rest of the building?"

Still shaking and gaunt cheeks pale, Mrs. Singleton nods. "Sure thing. What's it like out there, Chief? It's been something straight outta the bowels of Hell itself in here. I done seen awful things worse than any nightmare or scary movie could ever imagine. Been hiding here and praying my heart out, just waiting on my turn."

"Things are...difficult. We're rounding up as many as the place can hold here. For the time being, until this mess gets sorted out, we'll all be safe huddled here."

"What happened to them, Chief?"

Taking a deep breath, she leans closer and pats the frail woman's hand. "I don't have an answer, Mrs. Singleton. Let's concentrate on one thing at a time, okay?"

"Chief?"

She holds her breath, knowing what the question will be before even asked. A heavy sense of sorrow claws in her chest while scanning the old woman's features, afraid additional bad news would cause a heart attack or stroke, so she makes up her mind to answer with a bald-faced lie. "Yes?"

"Is Roger with you?"

Unable to look the sweet woman in the face while lying, she rises and heads to the side door. "No, he's helping rescue others, and a group of them will be here any minute. We'll talk later, once we're all safe. Okay?"

"Sure thing, Chief."

Ignoring the painful interaction, feeling like a huge ass for being so deceitful and the knowledge she killed Mrs. Singleton's only living relative, Regina opens the door. She helps Jesse gather Susie's limp body from the Humvee, making sure their movements and sounds of their footsteps on the concrete are quiet so they don't rile up the unwanted guests outside. The racket from earlier was loud enough to drive a crazy person sane.

Once back inside, they deposit Susie on a cracked, well-worn couch in the waiting room. Mrs. Singleton follows them, a cup of water and a few shop towels clasped in her hands. *Jingle Bell Rock* thrums from the speakers in the ceiling.

"Take that door right there." Mrs. Singleton points left. "It leads to the second floor. Take the stairs, and then the first door on the right leading back down. It comes out in sporting goods. That way, you won't make more racket messing with the gate."

Jesse reaches over and hugs the woman's neck. "Hey, Mrs. Singleton. Sorry to see you again under such circumstances."

With a wave of her arm, Mrs. Singleton brushes Jesse's hug away. "Ain't got time for pleasantries, girl. I'll tend to this here young one. You two get about dispatching the sick. Lord, I prayed for a miracle, and he delivered. He surely did. Now scoot!"

She exchanges glances with her daughter and a hint of a smile dances on Jesse's lips. Without a word, they disappear through the door and head toward the alternate sporting goods entrance.

"Grab a machete. We can't risk shooting them. It'll just draw more to the sound. Use both hands and swing with everything you have toward the head. Pretend you're carving a watermelon. Don't scream or make any noise. Can you do that?

Jesse's jaw clenches with anger and a hint of annoyance. "If it means making this place safe for all of us—hell yeah. I come from tough stock, remember?"

Letting go of the doorknob, she pulls Jesse into a bear hug. "If I haven't mentioned it already today, I'll say it again: I love you, and I'm so damned proud to call you daughter."

Jesse moves away and smirks. "Yeah, yeah. Say that again when other people are around to hear you, Mom. Let's get this over with. I know the code to lock the front doors, so let's make our way to customer service. I've gotta get upstairs and get the front doors locked before those things make it inside the store."

Nodding, she opens the door and the duo step out, Regina in front, Jesse right behind. Glancing both ways, ensuring they are alone, they crouch and dash toward the end of the aisle housing camping equipment. In the knives and tools section sits a freshly stocked display station full of cutlery-grade, stainless steel, molded grip machetes. She holds in a sigh of relief they aren't in plastic packages and instead, hangs from strips of leather attached to the handles. She nearly laughs at the bright words emblazoned on the front. "Perfect for use while riding horses, cars, trucks, and boats."

Hmm, no mention of how they'll stand up to slicing through craniums. Guess we'll find out soon enough.

She smiles as Jesse dangles a canvas backpack in front of her face. With quiet movements, they cram the bags full of blades before putting them on. On the shelf to her left, she notices several cans of safety air horns. Rather than questioning the reasoning for their odd placement, she snatches two up and motions for Jesse to turn around.

She stuffs them inside Jesse's pack. "I've got an idea. They are attracted to noise."

"Let's hope they hate Christmas music."

"Funny girl. Is there a window facing the front of the store from upstairs?"

"Yeah, but it's really small."

"I'll only need enough room to chunk these suckers out into the parking lot. The noise will draw them away from the door."

"Great idea! Let's go."

Blades in the air and footsteps quiet, they ease their way through the store. The sounds of faint whimpers from before is gone, and being inside the giant space with only holiday music and not bumping into frazzled shoppers is strange. Without the ding of registers, mumbled conversations of others, and even the occasional voice over the loudspeakers makes walking through the place feel foreign.

With every step, she swears the music grows louder. The bright, overhead fluorescent lights shine down on nothing but two scared women and the silent, unmoving stock on the shelves. A fleeting thought of whether the retail giant will ever be full of harried shoppers pushing overstuffed carts around makes her heart sink.

Nothing will be the same again. Ever.

They make it past the toy aisle but then Regina stops, motioning for Jesse to freeze. A familiar, yet out-of-place sound reaches her ears. Holding her breath, she peeks around the end display.

About ten feet away, crouching next to a center rack of vitamins, is a man dressed in the dark blue uniform of Malvern Police Department. It finally dawns on her the noise from earlier was from his leather Sam Brown belt while he moved to reposition himself. It doesn't matter that she cannot see his face because she recognizes the thick mop of curly dark hair, the black edges of a tribal tat peeking above the collar, and his broad shoulders.

Kyle Pender! Thank God!

His arms are raised, service weapon pointing toward the front. Even though the building is temperature controlled, droplets of sweat dot the back of his neck. Following the trajectory of the gun, she scans the area to see if Kyle's attention is locked onto yet another mangled corpse.

Seeing nothing but rows and rows of makeup, hair products, and medicine, she contemplates the best way to signal to him without making noise.

Turning back to Jesse, she holds a finger to dry lips, reaches past her, and grabs a small, pink stuffed bear from the shelf.

Jesse mouths, *"What's wrong?"*

Regina points to her chest. *"Cop."*

Jesse closes her eyes and nods, shoulders sagging with relief.

Squatting down, she takes another peek, thankful Kyle is still in the same position as though his boots are glued to the polished floors. With one swift move, she slides the pink toy across the floor. It stops less than a foot in front of Kyle.

The reaction is immediate. His head moves a fraction toward the bear and then over his shoulder. Knowing her face is a swollen, bloody mess, she waves, motioning for him to come their way.

Kyle's expression switches from fear to recognition and he lowers the gun. In seconds, boots damn near silent against the floor, he rounds the corner.

On instinct, Regina leans in and brushes her lips against his ear. "You okay?"

Kyle nods, his thick hair tickling her nose. He still smells like ginseng and cloves but with an additional undertone of musk from sweat.

"Any others here?"

He shakes his head and swaps positions, warm lips next to her neck. "Got 'em all gathered in the food locker in the back. I was heading to the front to take out those things."

She pulls away. "Don't. There's too many. Jesse knows the code to lock the glass doors. Follow us to customer service. I've got a plan to lure the bastards away from the entrance."

His head bobs in agreement and he moves ahead, taking point while Regina and Jesse follow in single file behind him.

As they draw closer to the front of the store, they hear the disgusting sounds from the entrance. The chomping, growling, funky-ass mewling bounces off the walls and high ceiling, amplifying the noise. The sickening sounds drown out Bing Crosby's *White Christmas*. Her stomach roils in protest. She imagines Jesse's reaction is even worse.

When the trio reach customer service, Regina looks back to Jesse. She points to the door on the right with a key code box. She taps Kyle on the shoulder, he stops, and Jesse moves to the front.

Regina stands guard, machete above her head like a baseball bat, eyes scanning the empty checkout lines. The sounds of Jesse punching the keys and the electrical *ding* when the correct code is entered seem as loud as if someone yells.

In seconds, they are upstairs inside the main control area. Jesse tries to move past Kyle, but he holds her back, motioning for her to stay put until the area is deemed safe. Regina locks the door behind them, and in practiced unison, backs pressed together, her and Kyle clear the room.

The only thing standing out that anyone had even been inside is an uneaten donut and cold coffee on the edge of one of the desks.

Regina lowers the machete, removes the satchel from Jesse's back, and grabs an air horn. "Okay, baby. Get ready. We're gonna make some noise and get those bastards outta here. Wait to punch in the code until my signal."

"Air horns?" Kyle rolls his eyes. "Oh, I've got a much better idea. Loud *and* bright."

Regina grins as Kyle produces a set of car keys from his front pocket. "Your unit out there?"

"Yep." Kyle moves to the small window no bigger than four bricks. "I'll hit the remote and they'll come lurching. Once they gather round, they'll be easy to pick off."

He reaches for his gun, but Regina stops him. "No. If you start shooting, the ones you don't hit will just come right back. Reed, Walt and Martha Addison, and a few deputies, will be here soon. They're heavily armed so let them take those monsters down. We've got to get back to automotive and be ready to open the bay doors when they arrive."

"Stop arguing!" Jesse snaps. "I'm gonna lock those doors in five seconds no matter which method of destruction you two pick. I don't want them getting inside!"

Knowing her daughter is beyond the point of being on edge, Regina steps back and nods at Kyle.

A grin of satisfaction spreads across his lips. "We'll compromise."

Raising the key fob, he clicks it twice. The wail of the siren makes Regina's heart pound with excitement, like a Pavlov Dog. Scooting next to Kyle's body, she stands on tiptoes and peers out the window.

Kyle's unit is decked out with extra blue lights and strobes. The entire black Charger is awash in a sea of blinding, white strobes, and azure-colored spinning lights. Inside the quiet room, the lone siren sounds like twenty.

Craning her neck to the left, she tries but cannot see the front of the store, but the limited perception doesn't matter.

The plan worked.

In seconds, a few lumbering corpses appear in her line of vision. Bloodied, battered, some missing limbs, others dragging broken legs and feet behind them, stagger toward Kyle's unit. She silently counts twenty just as Jesse taps out the code and seals the doors.

The hungry mass swarms the car, blocking the view of the vehicle in seconds. Bile burns up the back of her throat after realizing two of them wear outfits just like Kyle.

"Thank God!" Jesse punches the button, turning off the annoying Christmas music. She turns her gaze toward Kyle. "Okay, question: any of those things inside the store?"

He clicks the fob again and the blaring screech of the siren ends. Kyle steps away from the window and moves over to the closest desk, grabs an unopened bottle of water, guzzles half of it, and then takes a huge breath.

"Yes and no. Yes, there were, but I took care of them. Six of them were in pet care. Weird, huh? Guess they thought dog food was a good source of protein."

Jesse rolls her eyes. "That's not even funny."

Kyle ignores the snarky comeback. "Got the live shoppers to safety and then swept the rest of the store. We're good. Thank God only a few of those mad munchers decided to shop at Walmart today."

"Did you leave the dead where they fell?" Jesse whispers.

Kyle sighs. "Didn't have time to do anything else with them. Guess we'll need to move them somewhere proper rather than all over the floor."

"Oh, no way. I'd puke." Jesse blanches.

Regina notices Jesse is shaking, partly from being clothed in only thin pajamas, mostly from stress. Reaching behind her, she yanks a sweater from the back of a computer chair and hands it to her shivering child. Jesse gives her a weak smile while donning the thick covering.

"Don't worry, sweetie. We'll take care of the cleanup." Kyle looks over at Regina and grimaces. "Parker, you really need to do something about your head. It's bleeding like a stuck hog on a hot summer day."

Regina chuckles at his inappropriate humor. "Mad Munchers? A description that's pretty much on target. I wish people would stop commenting about my damn head. I'm fine."

He leans closer, gaze focused on the gash. "You don't look fine. You ain't—?"

"No, I'm clear." The question irritates her, and she takes two steps back. "A few grunts smacked me around when I tried to stop them from shooting unarmed citizens. We ain't got time for idle chit-chat, Kyle. How many people are in the back?"

"I counted fifty. Mrs. Singleton is the last straggler. As far as I know, she's still in automotive. Couldn't get her to budge no matter how hard I tried. She told me to go and lock the door and leave her alone. Stubborn old bat balled up her fist and punched me…in an area I'm sure she ain't touched in years."

The image of the old woman slamming her wrinkled fist into Kyle's junk flashes by, forcing Regina to stifle a laugh. "We saw her. Got her and another young girl squirreled away in the waiting area. We'll go get them out and meet you in the back. Everyone's gonna have a job to do. We've got more people coming. The military gave the orders to terminate everyone who hasn't been tested. We don't have much time. The troops plan on pulling out by noon."

"Say what?" The last remaining hints of color in Kyle's cheeks vanish.

"I'll explain it all in intricate detail later. We've got to move. It's gonna be rough trying to corral all those panicked people from the school and maintain some sort of control. Looting is a real possibility once they arrive here. Where's the rest of Malvern's finest? We sure could use some help."

"Chief Hollingsworth left for Colorado two days ago. Lt. Barker is in charge. He took three officers over to the hospital to help secure the place, but I haven't heard a word from him since they left the PD. Starkson and Kilpatrick are in the deer woods down near Poyen. I tried reaching them on their cells, but the calls didn't go through. Me, Trenton, and Gonzales were on our way to the nursing home on Sixth Street to take the elderly in for testing when we got a call from here. I made it—but as I'm sure you noticed earlier—Trenton and Gonzales didn't."

"Ain't many of us left, Kyle." Regina swallows the ever-present bile. "Sheriff Calhoun is gone, but Allsop and Bailey are with us. I don't know the status of the other deputies."

Kyle blanches and points to the door. "Good God, it just keeps getting better and better."

The trio head down the stairs when the rest of Kyle's words sink in. Regina freezes in midstride as though she ran into a brick wall.

"It's your head, isn't it?" Kyle produces a bandana from his back pocket and dabs at the gash.

Regina pushes his hand away. "Kyle, did you say Mrs. Singleton hit you?"

"Yeah, she was scared out of her wits. Called me some names I ain't even said before to my worst enemy."

Pale cheeks. Aggressive behavior displayed by one of the kindest, good-natured souls on the plant. Shunned Jesse's hug. Oh, shit! I didn't see any blood on her, but I didn't check for any bites or scratches.

"Mom? What's wrong?" Jesse whispers, instinctively moving closer.

"Change of plans. We've got to get to Susie. Right now."

Barreling past the duo, she races to automotive, hoping Kyle is right about the building being secure.

And praying her gut instinct about Mrs. Singleton is wrong.

Chapter 4 - Complete Power Failure

Saturday, December 20th – 11:35 a.m. – Eastern Standard Time

PRESIDENT-ELECT RONALD Krump's penthouse suite is a flurry of noise and activity. Though spacious and used to extravagant parties full of over-dressed New York movers and shakers, seeing it full of countless Secret Service agents in complete panic mode makes his stomach burn. He tries ignoring the din of mumbled voices as he opens the desk drawer and snatches a handful of antacids. The latest news—the unbelievable events—made his gut sour.

"I will not leave here until all of my belongings are packed!"

Collette's high-pitched voice is difficult to listen to on a good day, but in her current frenzied mood, the squeaky voice seems an octave higher. His wife isn't a woman to be trifled with when on a mission.

Period.

Whether it was finding the perfect outfit to wear with the correct shoes and accessories, or decorative decisions regarding the apartment, no one dared stand in her way. Being told they were to evacuate the home she'd spent six years of her life picking out every single item crammed inside sent Collette into an emotional meltdown.

If tabloid reporters were around, they would have labelled it a bitch fit.

He can sense Collette is about to snap.

Her thick, brunette hair, normally styled to perfection, is a horrible mess. Tendrils escaped from the chignon she created earlier and stick to her thin, damp neck. Without her entourage of stylists to transform her from meager to mega, she looks rough. The expression favored by his grandfather about cheap women numerous times when he was younger pops into his mind.

"That woman looks like she's been ridden hard and put away wet."

Extra Secret Service agents arrived less than twenty-four hours prior and caught both Ronald and Collette in bed. Collette was in a deep sleep induced by the handful of medicine she took every night. Ronald had crashed while working on his first-ever speech as the new President of the United States. When Agent Coleman woke them up with the dreadful news, both thought they were on hidden camera, a colossal joke played at their expense.

Looking around at the frenetic scene inside his home, he wishes it is a fictional prank rather than horrific reality.

His gaze settles on his wife. Collette—sans makeup—didn't have time to primp and preen herself when the agents broke the news about the outbreak. His tethered, other half of fifteen years fainted when the lead agent informed them the White House had been overrun, along with the Pentagon, CIA headquarters, and Wall Street. She was unconscious long enough she didn't hear the exact details of what was going on, and she still assumes a terrorist attack of some sort is the problem.

He could sit her down and explain the harsh, new reality, but he's struggling with the news himself and if Collette hears what is really happening, she will be a total basket-case. While she was still splayed out on the cool marble, he instructed the agents to remain quiet and not answer any questions she posed once she regained consciousness. Thankfully, once Collette revived, she'd been too preoccupied with packing up their belongings to ask questions.

He thinks about the parties thrown on election night and after the Electoral Colleges met and cast their votes. Though less than a few weeks in the past, it seems ages ago. His childhood dream of sitting in the Oval Office as Commander-in-Chief of the greatest nation on earth is only thirty days away, and the thought of never getting to fulfill the dream makes him furious. The dire situation is akin to losing, and Ronald Eugene Krump *despises* failure.

With no White House to lord over, he wonders what location they will be evacuated to, and so far, none of the agents have given a full answer, only repeating the same bullshit—they will go somewhere secure. Originally, the plan was to remain in the penthouse under heavy guard, and once the government contained the situation at the White House and Pentagon, move them to PEOC. When one of the late-arriving agents appeared hours ago, the plan changed. The man had been covered in blood and terrified, shaking as he retold the story about his escape and the utter and complete decimation of all high levels of government personnel. According to the agent, all of D.C. and most of the east coast were filled with thousands of reanimated corpses. The rest of the globe was in the same, deplorable state.

All the news was mind-numbing, but the one tidbit that nearly sent Ronald into a catatonic state was the CDC. According to Agent Coleman, the only hope to figure out what brought the dead back to life was gone. Somehow, several of the undead made it inside, and within three hours, the high-tech Atlanta facility was nothing more than an overpriced mausoleum.

His stomach churns and the antacids aren't helping.

So much for worrying about how to handle ISIS, immigration issues, the economy, healthcare, global warming, gun control, or violence in the streets. The world just collapsed in on itself. Will he even have a country to run before the nightmare ends?

He stands and moves through the throng of agents, all of whom ignored Collette's outburst. Most are too busy staring out the windows, watching the chaos unfold on the streets of Manhattan. The remainder of them lug suitcases out the front door, on their way to the roof.

"Collette, please do not worry. These men are professionals and will take care of our needs, including making sure our treasures are pampered and secured."

Agent Coleman, who's was assigned to guard them the minute Ronald won the Democratic nomination, scowls. "Sir, we aren't your local movers. We are here to gather essential items only. We leave in five minutes. The helicopter just landed on the roof."

Collette's eyes narrow into small slits. When angry, they turn from lime green to vibrant teal. A verbal explosion is about to spew from her silicone-plumped lips. Agent-in-Charge Coleman is seconds away from having about three pounds of his ass ripped off from a mouth full of enough dental work to buy a small house.

"How dare you! You do realize I'm the First Lady, right?"

Agent Coleman's face turns beet red, a thin sheen of sweat glistens on the top of his lip. He no longer wears his jacket, and the stains of perspiration discolor the white shirt under the armpits. Though he's been busy barking orders and instructions to the other men, he has yet to raise his voice to either of the Krump's.

Until now.

Coleman grabs Collette by the arm, shoving her toward the bedroom. "I am aware of your title, Mrs. Krump, but if we don't get you both out of here and safely underground, you won't have to worry about what expensive ensemble to wear to your husband's inauguration. Dead people don't concern themselves with such trivial events."

The look of shock on Collette's face would have made Ronald chuckle any other time. Her face is stretched tight from numerous facelifts and countless injections of chemical fillers. The only way to really tell if she is angry is the color of her eyes. Ronald is the only person who'd ever spoken to Collette in such a rude manner, and it never boded well when he did. Credit card charges skyrocketed, and their bedroom became colder than the grave.

Even though he agrees with Agent Coleman, he feels the need to come to his wife's defense. Coleman, please don't address my wife in such a rude manner."

"You truly are a pompous, arrogant buffoon! And you," Coleman's attention turns to Collette. "Are the most self-centered, fake, plastic-riddled bitch I've ever met. If I didn't love my country so much and ache for what's happening to her, I'd say I'm glad this happened before the likes of either of you defiled the hallowed grounds of the White House. It sickens me to no end that the rest of the succession line is dead. Even the Secretary of Homeland Security, who was nothing but a political puppet with no discernable brain power and a major coke-fiend, would have been a better option than you. Now, fucking move your privileged, lily-white asses out the door and up to the roof!"

The room falls silent. The stares of the others bore into him, making a flame of anger erupt inside his chest. It is one thing to dress down his overbearing wife, hell, almost comical, because quite frankly, everything Agent Coleman said to Collette is on target, but no one will get away with talking to him that way, not even amid a global crisis.

"Agent Coleman! Contain yourself. You work for us, remember? Apologize to my wife right now for such intolerable behavior or you're fired."

"Fired? *Fired?* Are you insane? No wonder the world is falling apart. It was full of idiots who voted in the King of Idiotic Morons to the throne!"

Collette's face blanches. Before Ronald can stop her, her wrinkled hand full of over a million dollars' worth of jewels reaches out and slaps Coleman. The *crack* as her skin connects with his cheek reverberates nicely off the acoustical walls.

Coleman's reaction is swift and harsh. Ronald doesn't even get a chance to blink before the man's balled-up fist slams into Collette's chin, knocking her backward almost five feet. She crumples into an unconscious ball on the cold marble floor.

"What in the hell is wrong with you?" Ronald finally manages.

Coleman points his shiny SIG Sauer directly between Ronald's eyes. "I said it's time to leave and I'm not kidding. Not another word or I swear we'll leave you two here and see how long you last before those flesh-eating mongrels smell the stench and figure out how to climb stairs."

The burning in his gut from earlier ignites into an inferno. He glanced over at Collette's limp body while two agents picked her up and headed toward the front door. Nodding once to Coleman, he steps back and grabs his briefcase from the desk. Coleman never lowers the pistol as they walk out the door and toward the stairs.

By the time they reach the helipad, Ronald is breathing hard. The sounds of the city under siege rise from the streets below. Smoke from other buildings in flames block out the morning rays of sunlight. Gunshots and the screams of terrified New Yorkers cause his skin to prickle in disgust.

But the noise he wants—yearns—to hear, is absent.

No sirens.

No emergency personnel racing to help the downtrodden.

Only screaming and gunfire.

Collette is already strapped into her seat. He climbs onboard and settles in next to her. Agent Coleman, and his weapon, veer off to speak with the pilot. Ronald takes the opportunity to stare out the open door to the city he loves more than any other place in the world. Manhattan has been his home, his domain, his kingdom, for over thirty years. A lump of tears swells inside his throat when he realizes the first two buildings he'd constructed are in flames.

He glances over at Collette, noting a bruise is already forming under her chin, and there is a large knot on the side of her head from when she hit the floor. He feels more concern and sorrow for the structures on fire than his own wife, and the reality of that hard truth adds to the numbness inside his soul.

What kind of man feels no grief for his wife, yet weeps like a child for a pile of metal and drywall?

His disturbing musings are cut short by two gunshots. He spins around in the seat just in time to see Coleman stumble and fall to the ground about three feet away. With his SIG Sauer still clutched in his hands, Coleman continued firing.

Ronald has no idea what he's shooting at, but it doesn't matter. On instinct, he leans down and covers Collette's body with his own, attempting to shield her from the bullets.

It is the last—and possibly first—act of kindness he ever does because Agent Coleman missed his target.

The agent screams yet it only lasts a split second, replaced by a gurgling, chomping sound.

Collette wakes up and wiggles from underneath him. "What the hell is going on?"

The appearance of the dead pilot answers her question. Ronald sees the entire world clearly for the first time in his life.

"The end," he whispers as the bloodied, drooling thing bursts into the cabin.

Chapter 5 - The Gathering

Saturday, December 20th – 10:45 a.m.

TURNER IS FULL OF raw, nervous energy. Too many thoughts zoom inside his mind, threatening to eat away any semblance of sanity.

He killed someone.

No, several.

Not a deer, or a hog, or even a rabid dog.

Human beings.

No, what once had been humans. He didn't recognize any of the others he'd shot except one—and the image, the smell, and the sounds—worm their way through his head like a barbed, two-headed venomous snake.

He'd known Raymond Wright his entire life; watched the kid skyrocket to local fame, heard the community buzz about scholarships and pro scouts skulking around the football games. He remembered him from school even though Raymond was only in the seventh grade when Turner graduated. Even back then, playing for the junior high team, Raymond Wright had all the makings, the physical and mental agility, to go far and maybe make a pro team.

Not anymore.

He ruined Raymond's chances of achieving football stardom with one bullet. He'd taken aim and fired, not even wincing when Raymond's blood, brain matter, and strips of flesh exploded less than five feet away from his position.

He'd seen the military descend on his hometown like a plague of locusts. Witnessed a helpless neighbor treated like treasonous criminal and executed in his own front yard.

Stephen Sikes was only fifteen when his life ended in a flash.

In front of his poor mother.

He'd been ordered at gunpoint by soldiers to leave under the threat of bodily harm. He'd watched the love of his life yanked away by the same goons while he'd be unable to stop them.

Seeing the videos Seth sent him earlier were awful, yet they paled in comparison to experiencing real people turn into flesh-eating creatures.

Taking them out will haunt his dreams forever.

He had played simulated, live-action video games all his life, spending hours upon hours with friends, stalking, shooting, blowing shit up, but the real world is harsh, cruel, and downright sickening. Virtual reality doesn't account for the horrid smells.

All those issues are bad enough, yet the one bothering him the most is the overwhelming anger burning inside his mind. He knows he won't hesitate again to kill one of the sick, and considering what they are dealing with, tries convincing himself the response is normal.

What scares him more than anything is he knows he wouldn't bat an eye if he kills a soldier. If one of them stands in their way of saving others or tries to hurt any of his loved ones, they'll be toast. The shift in his moral compass and willingness to commit murder to save another makes him wonder if he is in the early stages of turning.

Is that how the sickness starts? Your mind blocks out everything but anger and embraces hate? Jesus, how is this even happening? What's turning people into monsters? How does it spread? Why are some sick and others aren't? When will this nightmare end?

With the world turned upside down, he feels physically ill while following his dad, mom, and the others toward the gym. He spent four years of his life inside the familiar area, eating lunch with his friends, attending basketball games and school dances, and now, seeing the place full of terrified people and armed soldiers is surreal. How many residents had already been processed and deemed clear? Did they leave and head home, only to find the world they'd known their entire lives gone?

Did they even make it home?

Did the soldiers explain what was really happening or provide guidance or tips on what to watch out for, signs of contamination, what to do when confronted by a walking corpse?

"Son, you okay?"

The voice of his mother brings him out of his rambling thoughts. "Yeah."

"Jesse's gonna be fine. Don't worry."

He sighs as the group stops next to the double doors leading into the gym.

His father peeks through the doors. "Okay. Here's the plan. There ain't many troops left inside, maybe thirty or so. I'll go in first, alone, and gather them into a group. Once I do, y'all follow and surround them. We'll give them one chance to work with us, but if any balk or show signs of anything other than acceptance, we'll put them with the lieutenant and sergeants out back."

"Then what?" Bailey asks.

"I'll make the announcement we are taking our friends and neighbors to safety. No mention about the directive to kill them all. I mean it. No one is to say a word about it, not even to the soldiers. Looks like we'll have some help. I noticed Curt Campbell inside. He'll assist once he realizes we've got a plan."

"You serious, Walt? How in the world did Curt get caught?" Lamar asks.

"Judging by his attire and the way he's moving from one resident to the next, I'd say he had the same sort of idea as we do. Time to move out."

He watches his father enter the gym, heart pounding as a shiver of fear spikes while stepping forward and edging the door open with his boot. Seeing him march across the hardwood floor into enemy territory makes the breath catch in his throat.

He shudders. If they don't listen…

"Stop fretting, son. Your dad knows what he's doing. He's in his element now."

With a nod of his head, he acknowledges his mother's words of comfort while his gaze sweeps the men surrounding his father. Only one false move or hint of trouble and he will rush inside.

"Looks like Curt's spotted him!" Lamar whispers. "Looky there! Ol' Walt's got 'em eating outta his hands. They're all circling him like a hungry school of catfish on a wet lump of bread!"

Turner stiffens when the soldiers' close ranks around his father and Curt. Something inside his gut urges him to move. "Let's go."

Without waiting for a response from anyone else, he enters the gym. The others follow. His fingers grip the rifle with such intensity they are almost numb. Ignoring the low whimpers from several frightened residents as they pass by, he never takes his gaze off his father.

"Addy?"

The sound of a familiar voice—and his childhood nickname—causes him to stop in midstride. Glancing to his right, he confirms the identity. "Seth?"

Seth Montgomery picks his way through the crowd. His curly blond hair looks like he stuck his fingers in a light socket. Seth is almost three inches shorter than Turner and outweighs him by at least fifty pounds. Sweat trickles off his forehead and his Led Zeppelin t-shirt appears wet. He notices droplets of blood dot the front of the band shirt.

"You join the military?" Seth's voice is barely audible.

"No. Ain't got time to talk. Go back to your spot and stay put. We're here to get y'all out."

Seth's light blue eyes are wild with fear, and it's obvious he's been crying. "Those bastards killed Trevor! Shot him in the head at the house. Trevor flipped when they arrived, and—"

"Now isn't the time, Seth. We'll talk later. Promise."

The hurt behind Seth's eyes makes Turner wince on the inside, yet it cannot be helped.

His feelings about being rude to his best friend are cut short by his father's booming voice. "Because those are the new orders whether you agree with them or not! Now move!"

Leaving his bewildered friend, he raises the rifle while the others flank out and in seconds, they surround the troops.

"Lt. Pack gave us strict instructions to wait until the remaining troops arrive, then we are to…"

Turner shoves the tip of the rifle against the soldier's back who's standing toe-to-toe with his father. "One more word and it will be your last. You heard the man—move."

The gym goes silent. Electricity from hundreds of pairs of eyes staring at them fills the large space. Sensing a shift in command, the crowd of residents back away from them and part, leaving an opening for Turner and the others to lead the soldiers out.

The showdown between military and militia lasted only a few seconds yet seemed like an eternity. The one who questioned his father lowers his head, signaling defeat. Without saying a word, his father motions toward the kitchen and the group of soldiers walk across the floor. A low rumble of whispering spreads throughout the crowd as they move, most cursing the military under their breaths.

Once the last soldier steps through the doors into the kitchen, his father takes a deep breath. "Okay, here's the deal. If you want to keep your weapons and not be locked up, help us. The other option is set your guns down and join your lieutenant and sergeants under lock and key."

"Give up our guns? Are you insane? You do realize what's going on out there, right? In case you haven't, newsflash: the dead are walking around eating the living. The entire globe has been infected with some virus that kills at an unprecedented rate! We're trying to stop that."

"What's your name, kid?"

"Davenport, like it really matters at this point. Where's our lieutenant?"

"Still alive, I assure you. We ain't here to hurt no one. Enough of that is going on already by others." Walt answered.

"Then why all this? What do you want?"

"Y'all had orders to kill innocent people. *Our* people. *Our* friends and family. That ain't gonna happen. We know the world's gone to shit. We're completely aware of the collapse in Washington. Those people out there don't deserve to be exterminated just because y'all are afraid they *might* be sick. We're taking them to safety—someplace those infected can't get them—until all this blows over."

Davenport rubs his pale forehead. Turner notices a slight tremble in his fingers. "Blows over? *Blows over*? Shit, you are insane. This is the end. What part of that don't you get? It's like this *everywhere*."

The fury from before ignites inside Turner's brain. "We get it, you bastard. Your solution was to just kill the people you're supposed to protect then run out of town like whipped dogs! Dad—they aren't gonna help us. Let's lock them up right now."

"That's enough! All of you!" Martha's voice booms from the right. "The choices are simple. You help us evacuate those people or we'll leave you here without any weapons and let you fight off the monsters. You know, the ones I'm sure your employer created? Make your choice—*right now*!"

The kitchen falls silent as the group of camo-wearing men and women contemplate their next moves. The rumble of a vehicle approaching from outside causes him to glance out the window. His heart thumps while watching three Humvees roll up.

He returns his gaze to the soldiers inside, noting they heard backup arrive. He can tell they've made their choices, based upon the looks of relief and determination behind their eyes.

Curt Campbell puts the female in fatigues closest to him in a chokehold, a hunting knife the size of his forearm pressed against her exposed throat. "Time to decide is up. Drop your guns on the counter right now, or we'll pick them off the floor next to your dead corpses after I send this bitch off to eternity."

For emphasis, Curt exerts enough pressure to draw blood. The woman lets out a small whimper.

The sound of the automatic weapons clattering on the metal countertop fill the kitchen. Dejection and fear spread throughout the troops as they each raise their arms over their heads.

Except one.

Davenport.

Turner locks gazes with the fool and stares into the dark eyes of a man on the edge.

Just like me.

Everything happens in slow motion, like watching a movie unfold.

Davenport jerks the rifle to his shoulder, aiming at Curt's head.

Curt responds by slashing the blade across the woman's throat. Bright, red blood bursts from her neck, covering the front of her uniform and the floor. Her limp body sags in Curt's arms for a split second before he lets go and it collapses into a heap onto the kitchen floor.

Reed screams from his right. "Oh, shit!"

Red fury coats Turner's thoughts and he fires. The bullet rips through Davenport's left shoulder, and the force of the impact makes the man's body jerk yet doesn't stop him from pulling the trigger on his own rifle. A hail of bullets sprays out the end, the sound deafening inside the small kitchen.

The entire group of people, including Turner's family members, friends, and the other soldiers, drop to the ground. Davenport and Turner are the only two remaining on their feet. Though injured, Davenport clings to the rifle.

Turner steps closer and shoves the tip of his gun against Davenport's temple. "Drop it."

"What the hell is going on?"

"Freeze." Lamar answers the male voice from the doorway.

From his peripheral vision, he notices his mother and Lamar shift their weapons toward the door.

"Okay, okay. Let's not get all—"

"Shut up, grunt." Lamar grumbles.

Davenport lets his rifle fall to the ground. Anger mixed with pain swirls behind his eyes. Turner feels triumphant. "All of you—through that door right now!"

"I never forget a face. You'll pay for killing Martina. If it's the last thing I do, I'll—"

He doesn't give Davenport a chance to finish the threat. With precision and speed, he spins the rifle, clocking the bastard in the temple with such force Davenport flies two feet, landing with a hard thump on the floor. He's out cold and doesn't move.

"Well, that certainly didn't go as planned." Walt mutters. "Okay, you two pick him up and carry him through the door. The rest of you, get inside right now."

The kitchen fills with the sounds of boots tromping across the concrete floor as the remaining soldiers follow the orders, including the five new arrivals frozen in the back doorway. The garbage holding area is packed with close to thirty warm bodies.

"You can't just leave us here! One of my men is wounded. He needs medical attention!" Lt. Pack yells.

"Then you best use your field training and improvise, 'cause y'all are gonna be here for a while." Martha shuts and locks the door.

Satisfied the grunts are secure, the group make their way into the gym. All the terrified citizens huddle together in the middle of the room; several women clutch their children in their shaking arms. From the corner of his eye, Turner sees Seth and his parents to the right. The groups' fear and anxiety hang over the gym like a wet blanket.

"I'm sorry if we scared y'all." Walt's voice is calmer now. "We had to get them outta the way before we get y'all to safety."

Seth's dad, Clarence Montgomery, takes a step forward. "What do you mean, Walter?"

"Look, I ain't got time to tell the entire sordid tale. Let me sum up: things are bad, and right now, we've got to get everyone outta here. Chief Parker is at Walmart right now, setting the place up for us to hunker down in for a while. Need a show of hands—how many of you got your vehicles in the parking lot?"

About half of the group raise their hands in response to his father's question.

"Good. Okay, those of you with transport—step to the right. Those needing a ride, stay put."

A man Turner didn't recognize forces his way through the crowd and yells, "Why in the world should we listen to you? You stormed in here with guns drawn and yanked our protection away! We heard gunfire which means one of you shot a U.S. Soldier!"

"Hey, I ain't forcing nobody to do anything." Walt shouts. "You wanna go out there alone and fight off the walking dead on your own? Fine. Have at it. None of us are gonna stop you. Unlike those camo-wearing grunts, we're here to help you. Let me give y'all a bit of information before y'all make up your minds—things ain't the way they were before y'all walked inside this school. What's happening to our community is happening across the entire world, and I mean everywhere, not just the good ol' United States. Whatever has turned our friends and neighbors into hungry shells of their former selves is spreading faster than a stinky fart on a windy day."

Curt Campbell comes up from behind Turner and addresses the frazzled crowd. A collective gasp rolls through the group of citizens when they see the fresh blood on his clothes. "Mr. Addison is right, y'all. The phone lines are down, the Internet ain't functioning, and I overheard one of those guards talking on his radio earlier. They weren't gonna help us! They planned on—"

"Now's not the time for that discussion, Curt." Walt interjects.

"Wrong. We have a right to know what's really going on before we make any decisions!" a female from the crowd yells. Her defiant voice acts like a release valve on the others and in seconds, the cafeteria fills with the rumble of panicked residents, each yelling louder than the one standing next to them to be heard.

Turner cannot take anymore. He motions toward those with him. "Shut up! All of you! My family, these people, risked their lives to help you. You want to know what your precious fucking government was gonna do for you? Shoot you like rabid dogs. That's what Curt overheard. We did too.

Those bastards already proved their loyalty by barging into our town, yanking people from their homes, hell, even killed a few who didn't want to come. I saw one grunt take down a blind teenager in his own front yard."

The crowd lets out a collective gasp then falls silent once again.

Clarence Montgomery adds, "They killed my son in my living room. A fellow soldier, one who'd served his country and still bore the mental scars of his service overseas. Treated him like he was an enemy combatant and put three bullets into his head. I've known the Addison family my whole life. Lots of you have. Turner's right—the government ain't out to protect anything except the war-mongering suits in D.C.!"

"And ain't none of them left to give orders now, so we're on our own." Curt swipes a hand across his damp forehead. "Those men and women in green are trained killers with no leaders. How long do you think y'all would last with them? Here's the answer: less than two hours. By noon, all of you woulda been dead had we not shown up."

Turner nods. "Chief Parker and the rest of us agreed to step in and *save* you, offer a chance to escape and *live*, because it's the right thing to do. Like my dad always says, the world's gone to shit. If you want to survive the coming storm, then let us help you. We need to leave before the remaining troops arrive and find out we threw a monkey wrench into their plans."

Another man pushes his way through the throng of residents to the front. He recognizes him immediately. His head full of curly, gray hair, vibrant brown eyes, and the demeanor and patience of a saint, is clothed in jeans and a sweatshirt rather than his Sunday best.

Pastor Trent!

"Listen folks, we need to calm down. We've been praying hard for the last hour, asking God to release us from our captors and keep us safe. I, too, have known the Addison family for years. Walter, Martha, and Turner are wonderful, God-loving souls. When the Lord opens a door to freedom, should we stop to question why, or step through it in faith? My choice is faith. What's yours?"

A handful of people who raised their hands earlier indicating they had vehicles turn and flee the gym without a word, running as though prisoners who just discovered their cells are unlocked. Those who remain split off into two groups as requested.

Turner looks over at is father, who stands rock still, face beaming with what he assumes is pride.

"Those of you driving your own vehicles, wait until we're loaded up and follow us. Deputies Bailey and Allsop will escort you out front, in case we have unwanted company hiding in the parking lot. Let's roll, people. Time's a wasting. We've got to get situated and secure before night falls."

Pastor Trent claps his hands. "Amen, son. Amen. Darkness has stepped into the light of day, and its ugliness will only get worse when the sun disappears."

In minutes, the Humvees are packed with people and the caravan rolls out toward the front. Turner goes first, stopping to let Bailey and Allsop climb inside. Glancing in the rearview mirror, he gives the engine some gas and turns onto the road in front of the school.

A stream of vehicles, just like in a funeral procession, follow behind him as they made their way through the streets toward their destination. He forces his hands to remain steady while driving past mangled corpses and silently thinking, *Wally World, here we come. Please, Lord, let Jesse and Chief Parker be ready.*

And safe.

Chapter 6 - Harsh Reality

Saturday, December 20th – 10:46 a.m.

IGNORING THE PAIN thrumming from the wound to her head, Regina races through the aisles as toys, dog food, body lotion and cosmetics whizz by in a blur of colors and smells. She silently curses her stupidity for leaving Susie with someone she hadn't fully checked out.

If that girl dies because of my oversight...

The tread on her boots keeps her from sliding while rounding a corner leading into the sporting goods section. She hears Jesse and Kyle not far behind. Several displays in the middle of the aisle block her view of automotive.

The visual impediments do not matter. "Oh, my God! Nooooo!" Susie's shrill scream pierces the quiet store.

A dull *thump* follows the sickening, mewling sound Regina has come to despise.

Clearing the last visual obstacle, she pulls to a stop less than two inches from the metal bars. Behind them stands Susie, a bloody tire iron clamped in her shaking hands. The terrified girl doesn't seem to be aware of Regina's presence because her laser-beam focus is on what once had been Mrs. Singleton.

The old woman's blue smock is drenched in red from the large gash starting at the top of her head tracing all the way to the edge of her chin. The impact from the tire iron created a vicious wound yet hadn't stopped the old woman. She staggers back from the blow and then closes the gap between the two with a weird, halting gait.

"Get away from me! Jesus, somebody help me!" Susie screams while taking a swipe with the metal rod.

"Kyle! Shoot her!" Regina yells.

He bursts past her and stops inches from the gate. "Get down!"

The sound of his deep, booming voice spurs Susie to act. She spins around, dropping to the floor at the same time with the tire iron still firmly clasped in her hands. "Stop her! Please!"

Kyle raises his arms, firing two, well-placed rounds, both entering the old woman's forehead directly between the eyes. The velocity knocks her backward, blood and brain matter coating the highly polished floor and countertop.

Regina runs to the door leading to the stairs.

"Mom, don't!" Jesse yells.

Ignoring her daughter, fueled by fear and guilt, she keeps going. By the time she bursts through the door into the gated automotive area, she is out of breath. Susie is still crouched on the floor, arms over her head, sobbing uncontrollably. Jesse and

Kyle had knelt next to her on the other side of the gate. Bile rises in Regina's throat when looking at the destroyed mess formally known as Mrs. Singleton.

Her body had landed on its side, giving Regina a clear view of the lower leg. The tan khaki pants rose up enough she sees the imprint of scratch marks on the elderly woman's ankle.

Roger, I'm so sorry. Please forgive me for letting her turn into such a thing.

She gently touches Susie's back. "Are you hurt? Did she bite or scratch you?"

Susie jumps. "I...I...don't know."

"Here, let me look, okay? Breathe, honey. Just breathe. Talk to me. What happened?"

Susie sniffles and leans back against the metal gate. The poor girl is shaking so hard her teeth chatter. Regina sets the backpack to the side while studying every inch of Susie's body for any sign of contamination.

Susie wipes away the tears streaming down her cheeks. "I woke up and my jaw hurt. She was sitting there staring at me and didn't say a word when I tried talking to her. You know, to ask her what was going on, where I was, and where you were? I thought she was just a scared, old woman and too frightened to respond. I was thirsty and noticed the water fountain and went to get a drink. When I turned back around, she was on the floor, shaking. I...I...saw the cop and my aunt do the same thing so I knew what was coming next. I looked around for a weapon and found the tire changer thingy."

"Looks like you got a good lick on her." Kyle sets his gun down next to him and reaches his arm inside to offer a comforting hand to Susie.

Regina grimaces at him, thinking his remark was the wrong thing to say. "Did she touch you at all?"

Susie's eyes cloud over with fear. Red-rimmed from crying, they are nearly swollen shut. "No, but some of her blood got on me when I hit her. See?" She points to droplets on her shirt. "Oh, God! Does this mean I'll get sick and turn into one of them?"

Regina looks at Jesse as Susie drops her head down and weeps. Jesse returns the gaze, her own eyes welling with tears because they don't know the answer to the frightened girl's question. Fearing Susie will flip out, she bends the truth. "No, honey, I don't think so. From what I've seen, you must sustain a bite or scratch. You're clear, so come on, let's get out of here."

"I want my mom," Susie whimpers. "And I want to go home. Away from all this mess!"

"I know, sweetie. I know. Here, let me put this away and we'll get you outta here."

After easing the tire iron from the girl's grip, Regina stands and sets it on the counter. Jesse and Kyle continue murmuring words of encouragement to the distraught girl. Knowing they need to hurry and get to the back of the store before the others arrive, Regina decides to open the gate rather than take the stairs. Just as she reaches the button behind the counter, Kyle screams, "Susie, don't!"

Spinning around, Regina let out a gasp. Susie moved away from the gate, out of reach of Jesse and Kyle. Her mind spins with a million thoughts as

Susie puts the barrel of Kyle's service weapon against her temple. Their gazes lock and Regina sees the look of resignation behind Susie's swollen eyes.

"I want my momma!"

She lunges, legs pumping at full speed while Kyle and Jesse try reaching through the slats to stop Susie, but she is too far away from their reach, and from her own. The sound of the gunshot pales in comparison to the internal heartbreak inside her mind.

Unable to control herself or stop her trajectory, she cries out, "Oh, my God! No!"

Her body collides with Susie's, and they slam into the floor. Kyle's gun flies from the dead girl's hands, clanking across the floor. Hot, sticky gore sprays across Regina's face and chest before her head smashes into the slick concrete on the same side as the gash. The impact causes the bright interior of the store to dim, coinciding with loud buzzing inside her ears.

Susie's torso twitches once as blood pools around her head from the gaping hole where the bullet exited. Regina welcomes the moment of blurriness because she cannot stand the full clarity version of the limp body of Susie from Texas.

I promised to protect her. She trusted me and I let her down.

Overwhelmed by the image of the sweet, terrified girl blowing her head off, Regina cannot move. In the distance, she hears Jesse yell from her right, and the crackle of automatic gunfire from her left.

"Mom, that's gotta be Turner and Uncle Reed!"

Ae warm hand touches her shoulder. Kyle is right by her side. "Come on, Chief. We've got to let them in. Sounds like the things out back noticed them. We'll deal with this mess later."

On autopilot, she scoots across the floor, retrieves Kyle's gun, and hands it to him without saying a word or looking at the bloody mess from the two women. Kyle puts his arm around her shoulder, grabs her pack, and leads them away from carnage.

Mind numbed by the events; she forces herself to concentrate all her thoughts on helping the others as the trio make their way to the automotive bay doors.

If she dwelt too much on Mrs. Singleton, Susie, and the others she's killed, she will lose her fucking mind.

Chapter 7 - Time to Research

Saturday, December 20th – 11:46 a.m.

"DOC? YOU FINISHED with your hissy fit?"

Everett refuses to look up. Shame at his earlier outburst keeps his gaze locked on the gray wall, plus, he knows his eyes are swollen and red from crying earlier. He feels like the world's biggest wuss.

"Sorry about that. The first signs of dementia are sudden outbursts of anger."

Dirk steps inside the small room and leans against the edge of Everett's cot. "Yes, I'm aware, however, given our current situation, I'd say your response was quite normal. Don't try to weasel your way out of solving this mess by claiming you've lost your marbles. I won't buy into it."

"I'm not trying to convince you."

"Good, because it would be a waste of your energy. So, the guys are cleaning up the lab, which shouldn't take too long since they've got nothing else to occupy their time. No phones, the radio is silent, and they can't amuse themselves by playing games on the Internet. I'd say in about two hours, they'll be ready to go topside and get you a specimen."

Cutting a shocked and disgusted gaze toward Dirk, he snorts. "A specimen? You mean a former human who's turned into an unrecognizable thing? You're serious, aren't you?"

"Yes, I am. Recall I'm not exactly a jokester, Dr. Berning. Too many years in the military wore away most of my humor bone."

"No. It's a waste of time and too dangerous. I wouldn't even know where to start. Besides, I don't have the proper equipment here or the expertise to perform a pseudo-autopsy. I'm a scientist, not a doctor. I deal in microorganisms and chemical formulas. Med school was eons ago, and I only experienced cutting up a corpse once. Gross Anatomy was the only class I made a C in because I sucked at it. I'd just end up butchering the specimen like I did in school. Well, after I throw up first, which I did back then, too. My lab partner and instructor hated me the entire semester. They even nicknamed me Emesis Everett."

"Emesis?"

"Clinical term for throwing your guts up."

"Ah. Okay, well considering they're dead, I don't think they'll care how skillful your hands are or lack thereof."

"I certainly won't have to worry about family members complaining about shoddy work, but again, it won't matter. I don't have a clue where to start, nor do I have the proper tools to dissect a body. You need certain things to crack through bone."

Dirk sits on the cot and leans forward, face inches away. "Look, I know you're scared. We all are. I am not an expert in anything medical, but I know some things. The first one is I believe you can get a good handle on what's going on by testing a blood sample. Getting one won't require you to stick a blade through a torso or skull."

Despite the dire situation and subject matter, he chuckles. "You're right on that point. However, it would require me to get close enough to extract rancid blood. Newsflash: I'm squeamish. My aversion to blood and all the gooey innards of the human body was a major source of disappointment to my family. They all expected me to be a—oh, how did my father put it—ah yes, a *legitimate* doctor. However, suffering from emesis and syncope barred me from pursuing a career as a physician, much to the dismay of my parents."

Dirk furrows his brows. "Stop throwing out words I don't know. What is syncope?"

Rising, he walks over to the desk across the room. "It's the clinical term for fainting. Or, as my lab partner liked to say, passing the fuck out."

Dirk joins him, clapping a big hand across Everett's back. The man is strong, and he forces himself not to wince.

"Don't you worry, Doc. We'll handle the gooey shit so you won't take a swan dive. Porterfield and Warton volunteered to venture topside. Considering all that's going on, I doubt it will take long for them to find you a test subject."

"You aren't going to let this go, are you?" He sighs after swallowing a mouthful of saliva. His stomach roils.

"Nope." Dirk opens the door.

They walk down the hallway in silence for a few moments. An unanswered question from years ago resurfaces so before forgetting, he decides to ask. "Why was the project named Rememdium instead of Remedium? Dr. Flint never got around to telling me."

A sad, lonely smile crosses Dirk's lips. "Do you recall the conversation we had not long after I rescued you, when you asked me how I became associated with Dr. Thomas?"

Everett nods.

"Then there's your answer."

He recalls the terrifying tale of Dr. Thomas and Dirk in the jungles of El Salvador, and how Dr. Thomas lost his wife and children at the murderous hands of a madman. The answer slaps him in the face. "A play on words? In memoriam? For his wife and children? He wanted a cure found in their memory?"

This time, Dirk's smile is genuine. "See? You're the only one who's figured it out. Even Dr. Flint didn't know, which is why she never shared the answer with you. As I mentioned before, you're our only hope. I'm assuming you aren't a religious man, so instead of nicknaming you the new savior of mankind, I'll simply start calling you Obi-Doc-Kenobi."

"And you said you don't possess a sense of humor. Here's another newsflash: I may be a nerd, but I'm not a Star Wars fan. I've always been a Trekkie. And you're wrong about my religious views. Though I don't agree with any particular sect, I am one of the few who believe science proves we are a created species."

Dirk's eyebrows rise. "You continue to surprise me. I certainly never thought I'd hear you say those words."

"When I graduated college with my degrees, I was an adamant atheist. To me, nothing was real except physics, chemistry, and math. When people posed questions to me about life, death, humans having a sense of morality, among other things, I brushed them off as simple-minded fools. My perspective on life changed after my children were born."

"How so?"

"I stared into their faces, marveling at the immense complexity of the human eye. While in awe of just that one piece of anatomy, I felt a shift in my beliefs, though I never vocalized them. However, after losing my entire family, I cried out in despair, cursing God for taking my loved ones away. During my outburst, it dawned on me I was talking to an entity I didn't believe in. I wanted answers—needed to know what happens after we die—because I couldn't grasp the concept those happy, full-of-life individuals simply ceased to exist."

Dirk stops as they reach the door to the main lab. The eye scanner had been removed, allowing Dirk to push the metal door open. "Interesting. I'm still on the fence about numerous things myself. However, I am certain about one."

"And that is?"

"The dead can walk again."

"See? Something that makes absolutely no scientific sense yet, here we are, alive to witness the unbelievable becoming reality."

"What's happening hasn't changed your views? I mean, if you believe in some sort of divine creator then aren't you pissed off what he or she is doing to us?"

Everett grimaces. "How do you know it isn't our own mistakes with what was entrusted to our care that has fucked up the world?"

"I don't. That's where you come in." A shadow of sadness crosses Dirk's face. "Figure this out, Obi, before there's nothing left to save. I'm a little rusty on my Star Trek trivia, so forgive me if I butcher the phrase—but it's time you boldly go where no man's gone before."

Everett steps into the lab and watches the bustle of activity from the others as they buzz around the space, working in a collective harmony, surprised and pleased at how much progress they've made.

Without looking up, Kevin adds, "Screw prospering. I just want to live long. Get your motor running, Doc."

Chapter 8 - Settling In

"THAT'S EVERYBODY. We've got them situated in the bedding and outdoor sections. Curt's helping set numerous tents, the Addison clan and Jesse are coordinating water and food, and Pastor Trent got a head count. We're at two-hundred thirty, counting us. You need to hold still while Ms. Jane here patches you up, sis."

"My but aren't we bossy." Regina cuts her gaze to his, irritation spreading across her bloodied, dirty face.

Reed tries not to cringe at his sister's appearance, and it's impossible to look away from the ugly wound. He's not a doctor or nurse but knows she has a concussion from too many blows to the head and being unconscious for over thirty minutes while at the school. The dark circles under her eyes and lack of color in her cheeks make him worry about her health.

Those issues are bad enough, but what bothers him the most is the haunted look behind her eyes. The stress of the situation and the weight of her position and the responsibilities she shoulders make his tough sister look almost crazed. Regina's pushing herself way too hard, and the human body and mind are only capable of handling a certain amount of anxiety and trauma before rebelling.

Regina tries to walk away but Reed grabs her arm. "I'm not kidding. Sit down. The edges are turning red which means infection. While we still have access to fresh water and a surgical nurse, you're gonna hold still for a bit and let the others help. The crowd is antsy to hear from you, and they've already seen you looking like shit. You'll need to command respect and confidence when you address them because if they see any signs of weakness, it will only heighten their fears. No arguments."

"Fine. But don't think I'm doing this because you ordered me to. I'm doing this for Jesse and our freaked-out guests."

Ignoring his sister's smart mouth, he turns toward Jane Richmond. Seeing her lovely face, knowing she is still alive and near him, elicits a warm smile. Even though her gray hair is disheveled, and she wears no makeup, it doesn't matter because in his eyes and heart, Jane looks more beautiful and alive in her dirty scrubs. With hints of pink dotting her full cheeks, she's just as lovely as when they were in high school.

He'd been secretly seeing his high school sweetheart for the last three months and had worried about her safety. When he saw her in the crowd at the school, he nearly jumped out of his skin. "Okay, she's all yours, smart mouth and all. Can you slip her something to keep her trap shut for a while?"

"Brother—don't start. I'm exhausted and you're dancing on my last nerve, which is thinner than one of those wispy hairs on your head."

Jane motions for Reed to step aside. She examines Regina's ugly gash with careful, tender movements. "You two haven't changed one bit since high school. Still going at each other like two feral cats. Reed, don't you have someone else to rescue—or annoy? I've got a lot of work to do here and don't need her getting excited. I need her to hold still. Using the contents of a sewing kit as instruments will take a lot of concentration on my end. Oh, and probably a bit of pain on your end, Regina. Don't shoot me when the stinging starts."

He chuckles at the smug look on his stubborn sibling's face. She winks, acknowledging all is forgiven, and sinks into the lawn chaise he set up for her earlier. They both know the banter stems from his deep-seated worry about her health and safety.

Satisfied Regina is in good hands, he leaves the makeshift triage area near the pharmacy and heads toward the center of the store. The whispering voices of so many people converge together like collective cheers at a football game. Wincing at the loud noise, he picks up his pace. If they are to stay safe and hidden, at least long enough for the military to leave, the decibel level needs to be taken down several notches.

Movement to his right catches his attention. His muscles tense until realizing the form is Regina's secret love interest, Kyle Pender.

"How's the patient? Wait, let me guess: non-cooperative?"

"That's putting it mildly, Kyle. You know Regina—she's a pistol. Harder to handle than a slippery hog. Why you decided to take on the challenge of dating her I have no idea."

Kyle's eyes widen for a split second before he nods. "No doubt. Tougher than a wild razorback, too. Wasn't aware she told you about us."

Reed stops just shy of earshot of the passel of citizens. "She didn't. I'm just perceptive."

"Hmm, sort of like she is. Guess you're happy Jane's safe."

A grim smile tugs at the corner of Reed's lips. "Small town living. Gotta love it."

"With all the shit hitting the fan, I must admit I'm glad we ain't in a big city. I don't even want to imagine how tough others like us got it, trying to control thousands upon thousands of people."

"At the rate things are progressing here, I wonder if there's even thousands left to corral."

Instead of answering, Kyle turns his attention to the throng of residents in front of them. "I'm surprised our little group is semi-calm. I figured once they arrived here, they'd flip."

Following the cop's gaze, Reed sighs. "They're still in shock, Kyle. Right now, they're simply glad to be alive, but when reality sinks in, they'll freak."

"Doing my best to make sure that won't happen. I sent Bailey and Allsop to the front of the store with a roll of visqueen and instructions to cover up the glass doors. For a while, that will keep the visual of dismembered neighbors hidden. At least the glass will keep out the foul stench from their remains. While Jane is fixing up Parker, we should probably take care of the others in automotive and the six I bagged in pet care. They'll start stinking soon if we don't."

"Agreed, however, where in the world should we put their remains? The proper thing to do would be to bury them but that's too risky. No telling how many more are lurking outside."

Kyle rubs his unshaven chin. "I know it's morbid, but I was thinking put them in the dumpster outside and burn them? The heat would kill any remaining contagion, don't you think?"

Reed chews on his lower lip while considering the options. Unfortunately, no plan is perfect. "We still don't know what's causing all this, so I'm a bit concerned about burning bodies. What if the heat doesn't destroy the sickness and it's carried in the smoke?"

"Parker said that was the military's plan back at the jail."

"Then that settles it—I say we don't trust any plan those bastards put in place. I noticed a refrigerated trailer out back that looked like it had just been unloaded of merchandise. Let's move them there and keep the trailer doors locked tight until we learn more about what's going on."

Reed watches a group of about ten children, all appearing under the age of eight, sitting cross-legged on a giant pile of multi-colored pillows. Amid all the chaos and upheaval, they aren't deterred from playing. Someone has provided them with coloring books and crayons from the toy department, and in silence, they shut out their fears by applying vibrant hues to the grayish-white pages.

Kyle nods toward the lawn-and-garden department. "Let's get us two wheelbarrows and some tarps."

The duo turns and head right, winding their way through the aisles in silence. After procuring the tools necessary, including two safety masks and gloves, they journey toward automotive.

Things had been chaotic when the convoy arrived earlier. The unwelcome interaction with over twenty of the dead freaked everyone out. Stopping long enough to take aim and fire, it took the group several minutes to clear the parking lot. Then, they had to usher the terrified citizens inside before they became a meal if some residual corpses were hiding, so he hadn't had a chance to learn what happened to Susie.

When he asked Regina about the girl as he led his bleeding sister to the pharmacy, the only response she gave him was a solemn shake of her head.

He knew from the dejected look on her face the girl hadn't survived. "What happened to Susie?"

Kyle swears under his breath. "It's my fault, though I think Parker decided to put the heavy burden on her shoulders. I made a stupid, rookie mistake. Set my gun down close enough for the girl to grab through the metal slats. She was attacked by Clara Singleton. Susie took a tire iron and damn near split the old gal's head in two, but it didn't matter none because Clara kept coming. I shot Mrs. Singleton and then Parker ran inside. She tried to comfort Susie, but it was no use. She was beside herself. I heard a noise behind me, turned around for a split second, and the girl snatched up my gun. She blew her brains out right in front of us all."

Reed shakes his head in disgust. "Dear Jesus, God in Heaven. Had the girl been bitten or scratched?"

"She said no, but then she noticed blood on her shirt after splitting the old broad's skull. I think that's what sent her thoughts over to suicide. She feared contamination."

"Fear seems to be just as contagious as whatever the hell we're dealing with right now."

"No doubt."

They are only a few aisles away from automotive, yet the distance doesn't matter because the sour, rank stench of death lingers in the recirculated air. The foul, coppery odor of dead tissue and blood makes his stomach lurch.

Kyle clears his throat. "Let me go inside and open the gate. Should make this easier if that's even possible."

"You sure?"

"Yep."

The young officer disappears through a small door to the left. Closing his eyes, he tries to control his breathing, but the odor of rotting flesh brings memories back from the first time he'd seen dead bodies.

He'd only been with Border Patrol for less than a year when a concerned citizen called and reported an abandoned semi-truck about eight miles from the border. Reed accompanied two others as backup, naively assuming they would find a delivery driver with a blown tire.

He wasn't prepared for the truth.

When the SUV they were riding in topped a small rise, a horrible, rank odor wafted across the desert. A dilapidated vehicle that looked as though it had been driven through a battlefield, so dirty its original color was undiscernible, rested in silence over fifty yards away.

Sgt. Reardon extracted masks from the glove box and handed one to him, facial expression harsh. "Welcome to the real world, Newberry. You're about to see what happens when illegals hitch a ride with someone they don't know. They pay some bastard claiming to offer a better life across the border then get dumped off like yesterday's garbage."

Unwilling to show any fear or hesitation, Reed never said a word as they made their way to the back of the truck. When Reardon opened the doors, the sights and smells of thirty rancid bodies overrode Reed's bravado. When his shocked gaze landed on three children at the feet of a woman, their thin arms entwined with each other in a last-ditch effort to offer comfort to one another, his stomach revolted. He spent the next ten minutes throwing up behind a mesquite tree, fighting the tears of disgust and sadness with each retch.

The sound of the metal door opening brings him back to the present. After securing his mask, he pushes the wheelbarrow until he reaching the automotive entrance, stopping next to Susie's stiff body. The blood and fluids from her wound had turned dark crimson. One shoe is missing, and her shirt is coated in dark mahogany.

"Let's get her first. We'll need to be careful with Mrs. Singleton." Kyle's voice is quiet; reverent.

Nodding, Reed grits his teeth as the two men work in tandem, wrapping the girl's body in the black plastic tarp and hoisting her light frame into the wheelbarrow. After spreading out another large section of the visqueen next to Mrs. Singleton, Reed shoves the disgust at her appearance down deep and grabs her legs.

Kyle put his arms under her shoulders and together, they roll her onto what will be, at least temporarily, her grave shroud. "I've seen a lot of dead people in my day, but never anyone who looked like this. The color of the skin and all those weird, bluish lines over her body? Disturbing doesn't come close to describing it because it almost looks like roots took up residence underneath her skin."

Reed bites his lip. "The eyes—the way they turn solid black—that's what gets me. Well, and the fact they crave flesh. I hope whatever this shit is ain't airborne."

"If it is, then Walmart will be crawling with undead shoppers interested in nothing offered on the shelves."

"I see why my sister is drawn to you. Your sense of humor is just as twisted and sick as hers."

Kyle rolls the remainder of the plastic over Mrs. Singleton's corpse. "You know what they say about humor—it's insanity's next of kin."

He looks around to ensure they are still alone. Satisfied no one followed them, he grabs the handles and pushes the wheelbarrow forward. "We should keep to this back aisle so no one sees us. Let's get these two situated in the trailer then get the others. It's gonna take a few trips to remove six bodies."

A sick chuckle from Kyle makes him turn back around. The look of sorrow and disgust on the man's face gives him pause. He can tell Kyle is struggling to find words to express his thoughts. Kyle's facial muscles quiver while he grinds his teeth.

After swallowing twice, Kyle finally whispers, "We can get them in one trip. Three of them were children."

God help us.
Children.

Chapter 9 - Hunting Season Ends

Saturday, December 20th – 2:00 p.m.

SHAUN KILPATRICK FINISHES loading his trophy buck, securing it to the back of the four-wheeler. The morning's frigid air had been vanquished by warm sunshine. Taking off his gloves to finish tightening the rope, he is thankful his fingers are no longer frozen. A smile tugs at the corners of his mouth when he thinks about how jealous Emmett Jefferies will be when they roll up to camp. The beautiful specimen is Shaun's last tag for the season and Jefferies had yet to shoot one.

"What's so funny?" Jared Starkson asks.

"Oh, just prepping myself for the look of irritation on Emmett's face. He's gonna be pissed I won our bet."

Jared laughs and it sounds louder than normal in the quiet woods. "You may have won but I'll bet you he ain't gonna pay up. The man's tighter than a virgin's asshole."

"True, but you know, it ain't about the money anyway. At least not for me. I just love making him mad."

"Yeah, I get that. You ain't changed none all these years. You're worse than an old woman, holding onto a grudge for something that happened ages ago."

Shaun snorts. "You'd be singing a different tune had Emmett porked your girlfriend on prom night and in your own car."

"Probably. The difference between the two of us is I wouldn't still hang out with the douchebag. And I wouldn't be a cop since I'd have a felony arrest record for assault. I'da beat the fucker to a pulp."

"Like I said, I enjoy tormenting him every chance I get. You know, showing him how much more of a man I am than he is, or ever will be. Tormenting lasts much longer than a beat-down."

Jared shakes his head while climbing onto his four-wheeler. "Ah, the age old 'my dick is bigger than your dick' game. Gotcha. Say, while we're on the subject of tormenting others, want to explain to me why you haven't kicked Craig out of the club yet? I mean, we're risking a lot by having him here. What if he slipped and brought some shit here? We could lose our jobs."

"You really suck as a friend sometimes. Craig just lost his way after Sabrina died. Would you still be as harsh with your criticism of him if it was the bottle he hit—like you tend to do—rather than cocaine?"

"Doesn't matter because that ain't what happened. Booze is legal to buy. Coke ain't. End of story."

"Craig's been clean for three months now, so stop worrying. He needs the support of his friends, not condemnation."

"Will you use that same argument with the Chief? If so, I guarantee you it won't work. You gotta let that thin skin of yours toughen up and stop being so nice to others who can fuck-up your world in a flash. That's why after we get back to camp, I'm heading home. Already got enough meat for the rest of the year, and I don't want to tempt fate any longer. Craig's a liability."

Ignoring the taunt, Shaun settles onto his own machine after taking a picture of the fifteen-point buck. He clicks over to Facebook and tries to upload it, but nothing happens. The little blue ball in the corner continues spinning. "Damn woods! No cell service."

"You and social media. You're almost as obsessed with it as you are with Marian. Oh, and speaking of her, what's going on with you two? Rumor around town is your unit's been seen at her office several times in the last week. Please tell me that's not true. I can't take any more of your bitching about her and her shenanigans."

Shaun grimaces at the mention of his estranged wife. "Gee, and I thought that's what friends are for. Guess I was wrong. As I mentioned, your friendship skills are sorely lacking."

"Give me a break. I've endured way above my quota of listening to you dissect your relationship.

You married fools are the reason I stay single. You said after she cheated on you and got pregnant by another, you swore the marriage was over. What's changed now? Did she learn how to give a better blowjob or agree to a three-way?"

A flame of anger ignites inside his gut. "Watch it, Starkson. That's my wife you're talking about. We're working things out. We have no choice."

Jared raises an inquisitive brow. "There are always choices, Shaun. What…oh, shit. Please tell me it ain't yours?"

The anger from seconds ago dims while recalling recalled the last discussion he had with Marian and her gynecologist. He hadn't told a soul about the results of the DNA test since he found out two days prior. "Yeah, it's mine."

Jared's dark brown eyes widen in shock. "Oh, shit. That does change things. If it were me, I'd already skedaddled out of town."

"Believe me, I was so shocked, a kitten could've knocked me over. I'd convinced myself it wasn't mine. Still sort of numb about the whole thing. Can't believe I'm gonna be a dad."

"Wow—me either. You're a better man than me, Kil. Even if it was my bun in the oven, not sure I'd want to turn on the stove someone else has been cooking at."

Despite the intense subject matter, Shaun cannot stop himself from laughing. His best friend since second grade has a sick sense of humor. "That's why you're the whore-dog and I'm the loyal retriever."

"So, when does this little bundle of joy arrive?"

"Due date is January 26th. Oh, and in case you're interested, it's a girl."

Jared lets out a low whistle. "Let's hope she takes after the loyal retriever side of the tree, not the—"

"Enough, Jared. Again, that's my wife and child you're talking about."

The conversation ends abruptly as gunfire breaks the silence of the woods. The sound of weapons discharging is common during deer season and isn't the reason they both freeze. What transforms the two friends from carefree hunters back to concerned cops is the number of shots, followed by the screams of grown men.

Exchanging glances with Jared, he sees the worry he feels on the inside beaming across his companion's face. They fire up their rides and fly through the woods back toward camp.

Shaun tops the hill and stops, turning off his four-wheeler. Jared does the same. "Let's go in on foot."

They both reach for their rifles and dismount, creeping through the dense underbrush toward the encampment. The duo has spent every hunting season in the same woods for over twenty years and know every inch of the area.

The woods are bathed in complete silence. No chirps from birds or squirrels, not even the usual din of insects. As they pick their way closer, Shaun strains his ears for any sound. The gunshots ceased, as well as the screaming, and the stillness is almost more terrifying than the noise.

When they reach the edge of the camp, their original concerns morph into fear.

All the camping chairs surrounding the fire pit are overturned, food and utensils left where they'd been dropped. Impressions in the dirt indicate a lot of activity.

"What the hell?" Shaun mutters.

Jared creeps over and lets his hand hover over the ashes. "Cold. Been out for a while."

Shaun eases over to the front porch, drawn to the disemboweled torso of the twelve-point buck Craig Jackson shot earlier. The thing had been ripped to pieces and strewn from end to end of the fifty-foot porch. Nothing is left of it but skin, antlers, and bone.

Glancing up, he searches the area and counts all the vehicles. Sixteen—just like when they left—yet none of their hunting buddies are around. A cell phone is face-up on the ground, the edges coated in blood. Peering closer, he notices the last number dialed was 9-1-1.

The front door to the eight-room cabin they all share is wide open, and several sets of bloody footprints lead inside. The bay window has been shot out and shattered glass glistens in the afternoon sun.

"All their buggies are still here, too." Jared whispers from Shaun's right.

The hair on his neck stands erect when something gold and shiny catches his eye.

Then another.

And another.

The empty shell casings leave a trail from the front porch into the interior. Shawn snaps his fingers and points. Jared's face blanches upon seeing the vast amount of spent ammunition and blood spatter.

Both men slip into cop mode and sweep the cabin, keeping their steps tight and quiet while following the trail of bullets and blood. When they reach the back door in the kitchen, bloody handprints on the floor, walls, and doorknob greet them—along with an open door and a strange, chomping sound from the left on the back porch.

Shaun recognizes the noise first and mouths, *"Bear?"*

Jared looks at the amount of blood pooling on the floor by the back door and shrugs his shoulders.

Holding up his fist, the signal to remain still, Shaun takes a long step backward and peers out the small kitchen window to get a better view out back. Fearing his fellow hunters are victims of a four-legged predator, he needs to see exactly what they are dealing with—and how many. Black bears are abundant in the area, and maybe a family of them had stumbled upon the camp.

Time freezes as Shaun's brain registers the incoming signals from his eyes. A wave of dizziness hits him hard, and for a second, he sees double of the disgusting sight.

Craig, what are you doing? Why are you eating Frank's stomach?

Unable to contain his thoughts, he mutters, "No way."

"What is it?" Jared steps forward toward Shaun's position

It is the last words Officer Jared Starkson, the forty-three-year-old best friend of Shaun Allen Kilpatrick, will ever say, because as the words leave his mouth, Craig Jackson leaps into the kitchen, lands on top of Jared, both men fall to the ground and Jared's gun clatters across the floor. In shock, Shaun hesitates for a split second before firing. The bullet rips through Craig's shoulder but doesn't stop him.

Jared's screams gurgle to a stop when Craig opens his bloody mouth and latches onto Jared's windpipe, tearing it out with one bite. Jets of red arterial blood spray from the wound almost two feet into the air, coating Shaun's legs and the kitchen floor.

Taking a deep breath, he aims and fires again, this time hitting Craig's thigh. Blood and flesh burst from the wound, but Craig never gives any indication he feels a thing.

Jared is no longer fighting to survive. His limbs convulse from the enormous loss of blood. Only seconds remain before he dies, so Shaun raises the barrel, blows Craig's head off. The bullet exits Craig's skull and enters his best friend's.

"Oh Jesus—oh, Jesus! What in the hell?" He mutters while staring at the bloody mess in front of him, unable to grasp he just killed two of his friends with one shot.

The question is answered by the appearance of Frank Wilson's mangled body. Unable to walk since both sets of thigh muscles are gone, Frank pulls himself into the kitchen by grabbing onto the edge of the door frame. Shaun's stomach juices burn the back of his throat upon noticing a thick smear of intestines and blood left in the dead man's wake.

Frozen in horror and shock, he cannot believe what he's seeing. Frank's eyes are solid black and a strange pattern of blue lines reminding him of a road map covering his face and exposed arms.

His wits return after Frank opens his mouth and lets out a spine-chilling growl.

On autopilot, Shaun raises the rifle and fires, piercing Frank's skull just above the bridge of his nose. With one last gurgle, his former friend's head slams into the wood floor with a loud *thump*.

Noise outside catches his attention, so he steps over the corpses on the kitchen floor, rifle steady, and looks out the open door.

Unable to form words, mouth limp at the sea of blood and flesh littering the backyard, he stares in disbelief at the fourteen bodies in various states of dismemberment strewn across the dead, dry leaves. The ground gleams crimson underneath the mid-afternoon sun's rays, and the only way he can tell they are his friends and hunting buddies is from their torn clothing.

When he realizes two half-eaten bodies are still moving, he's hit with another bout of dizziness.

Stepping back into the main part of the cabin, he forces his fingers to quit shaking so he can extract his cell. He needs to call for help and prays the sporadic cellular service will work.

It doesn't. He is greeted by a robotic, droning voice: *"We're sorry. All circuits are busy. Please try your call again later."*

"That's for land lines, not cell towers!" He roars into the mouthpiece.

With no choice left but to leave and get help—or at least get closer to a functioning cell tower—he pulls the key from his pocket. Adrenaline pumps through his muscles as he runs out the front door, across the yard, and to his truck. Nerves on edge and mind spinning, he fumbles to open the door.

Once inside the cab, he sets the rifle in the seat next to him and tries inserting the key into the ignition, but it slips from his fingers and clatters on the floorboard. "Dammit!"

Bending down to retrieve them, the weird grunting sound he heard Craig mumble earlier hits him from the right. Snatching the key from the floor, he shoves it into place and the engine roars to life. The growing sense of dread doesn't stop him from glancing out the passenger window.

"Holy fuck!"

The once-familiar face of Martin Lawson stares back at him through the glass, eyes the same as the others., and the ebony nothingness is like staring into the pit of Hell. He can see Martin's white cheekbones and the upper part of his teeth where the soft flesh had been ripped off. The sickening sight is like a magnet, pulling all of Shaun's attention to the gore. The pull breaks when Martin's bloodied hands slam against the window, cracking the glass.

"Enough of this shit! I'm outta here!"

Throwing the truck into reverse, he tromps the gas and in seconds, is racing down the narrow, dirt road leading him away from the carnage at deer camp. He never lets up on the gas and makes the three-mile, bumpy journey to Highway 270 in record time. The gravity of the situation causes tears to slide down his cheeks. Inside the quiet cab, he offers silent prayers for the men he'd been friends with his entire life.

After the fourth mile, he tries the phone again and gets the same results.

Willie's Pit-Stop is less than half-a-mile away and he knows the owner will allow him to use the phone. He pushes the Ford F-150 hard, zooming down the empty two-lane highway at over ninety. Jerking the wheel, he pulls into the parking lot and slams on the brakes, leaves the truck running, jumps out, and dashes inside.

"Malvern police official business. I need to use your phone." Shaun looks around the quiet store for an employee and is greeted by silence while making his way toward the counter. "Hello?"

Gut instincts honed from years of being on the force kick him right in the stomach. Slowing his pace while inching closer, scanning the dimly lit interior, he is less than three feet away from the cash register when the stench hits him. The thick odor of copper and the odor of eviscerated bowels make him hold his breath.

Death.

The floorboards creak underneath his weight as he steps over and peeks behind the counter. His ragged breath catches in his throat.

There isn't much left of the old man. Willie's white hair looks as though it has been dipped in a can of red paint. The cavity holding his internal organs is nothing more than strips of flesh and rib bones. Clutched in his right hand is a Ruger and a spent shell casing rests near his head, inches away from a gaping hole on the other side.

God, I hope you blew your brains out before...

Backing away, he moves over to the cash register where an ancient, black rotary phone sits in the exact same place it has been since he was a boy. Willie Hopkins was too cheap to purchase a new one. Shaun hadn't seen anyone use the old thing in years and hopes it still works.

Picking up the dirty receiver, he winces.

No dial tone.

A grumble rises from the backroom Willie uses—well, used—as the office. After what Shaun experienced in the cabin down in Poyen, he doesn't feel the need to see what is making the noise.

He'd bet everything he owns he already knows.

Racing back to the idling truck, he jumps, floors the accelerator, and heads toward Malvern. Dead, leafless trees zoom by in a blur of gray as the speedometer nears one hundred. When he passes the road sign noting Malvern is only five miles up ahead, he tries his cell again.

Dead air.

"What in the hell is going on?"

A thousand thoughts race through his mind at almost the same pace as the speeding truck. In minutes, he crosses the city limits, hitting the brakes when coming upon a blockade of military vehicles obstructing the entrance to downtown.

"Shit, this can't be good." Shaun slows the truck down for a better look.

A large group of people covered in blood and gore ambled toward the county jail, some in uniform, some not. On instinct, he tromps on the gas pedal, forgetting all about Jared, Craig, Frank, Willie, and the others while dodging the dead.

All he can think about, what consumes him now, is getting to Marian and their unborn daughter.

By the time he drives through town, he understands things are much worse than he imagined back at camp. Hundreds of dead bodies and abandoned vehicles litter the streets. While dodging them, he realizes the rifle in the seat next to him isn't near enough protection from whatever is going on.

Spotting an empty Humvee up ahead, he pulls next to the driver's window. Making sure no one— *or thing*—is close enough to hurt him, he rolls the window down and peers inside.

The front seat is covered in dried blood and brain matter. A female in fatigues lays motionless in the passenger seat, half her head in the driver's side, frozen fingers still wrapped around the grip of her rifle.

Scanning the rest of the vehicle, he's hit with a spark of hope because three, fully loaded assault rifles rest near the middle console, and the key is in the ignition.

He glances around once more, making sure he is still alone. Satisfied he has enough time to check, he crawls partially through the opening and turns the key, ecstatic as the Humvee rumbles to life. A half-tank of gas remains.

He slinks back into the cab of his truck, grabs his hunting rifle, and backs the vehicle about four feet, rolls up the window, shuts the engine down, locks the door, and runs to the passenger side of his new ride.

"Sorry about this...and for how you died." He mumbles to the dead soldier.

Wincing at the rank smell and heartbreaking sight, he grits his jaw and pulls. Unwilling to leave her in the middle of the street, he drags the stiff body to the edge of the curb.

A grumble to his right makes the hairs over his entire body stand. He knows what it is and has no need to look. Instead, he turns and races back to the Humvee, climbs behind the wheel, executes a U-turn, and heads into the main part of town.

He makes it less than two hundred feet before the quiet afternoon fills with the faint sound of a siren. He slows and feels around for the assault rifles, overcome with the need to have them close and ready.

His hand touches an unfamiliar shape. He stops, craning his neck to see what it is. His mouth gapes open—a rocket launcher. Why in the world did the soldiers bring...oh, shit. They planned on some major destruction.

The familiar sound of automatic gunfire makes him break out into a cold sweat. The steady stream of pops drowns out the blaring siren.

Rubbing his forehead, willing himself up from what he prays is a crazy dream, he stares in horrified silence, temporarily frozen from unbridled fear.

Chapter 10 - Bracing for Impact

Saturday, December 20th – 2:10 p.m.

"WE TOOK CARE of the bodies in automotive and pet care. Jesse and Turner got all those under twelve in the toy section. They're all busy playing with toys. The rest of the group is waiting for you in bedding. Jane did a fine job on your head. Looks much better."

Regina glances over at Reed then at Kyle. Both men look as rough as she feels. Every inch of her body throbs, her head the most. She senses her brother has something else on his mind as they walk toward the center of the store. He hands her a bottle of water which she appreciates. After taking several gulps, she returns it to him. "What aren't you telling me, brother?"

In mid-stride, Reed stops and so does Kyle. "We've got a few…problems we need to tell you about before you give your little inspirational speech to the frenzied masses."

She rolls her eyes. "We've got a multitude of shit to deal with and today seems to be the day problems decided to come out of the woodwork. Spill."

Kyle peers over her shoulder, making sure they are still out of earshot of the others. "The first one is we've got three pregnant women on our hands."

"Oh, joy. Who? And how close to popping are they?"

"The first two I don't know. According to what they told Jesse, one is in the first trimester, the other in the second." Kyle grimaces and leans closer. "The third one is Marian Kilpatrick. She's due in a month."

Puffing her cheeks, she lets out a huff of air. "Shaun's wife?"

Kyle nods.

"Well, at least that gives us time to…"

"Actually, it doesn't." Reed cuts her off. "With all the stress of this nightmare, Marian started having contractions."

"Did I hear that right? We've got someone in active labor?"

All three turn at the sound of Jane Richmond's voice from behind them.

Reed waits until Jane joins the huddle "Yes."

"How far apart are they?" Jane wipes blood from her hands onto an already stained shirt. "And when is she due?"

"About seven minutes, and next month. Martha Addison made her a makeshift bed from piles of memory foam at the end of aisle six." Kyle points to the left. "The poor woman is scared out of her wits. Keeps asking for us to find Shaun."

"Jane, will you join Martha and keep watch on Marian for a while, at least until we can get her to the hospital?" Jane nods so Regina continues, "Reed, you mentioned we have more than one problem? What else is wrong?"

"Ain't no way to say it nicely, so here goes— Curt Campbell killed a soldier at the school. Slit her throat in front of thirty others. Things got dicey for a few minutes before we got a handle on the military."

"Was Curt defending himself, or did he just snap under the stress?"

She already knows the answer. It worms around in her gut like a coiled snake. Curt Campbell is a mean, cruel man, one she'd arrested twice for abusing his dogs. He is the kind of man the rest of the world pictures when the words *backwoods redneck* comes up in conversation.

"Cold blooded murder. Man's always been on edge and has a huge grudge against the military." Reed sighs. "He just used the situation as an excuse to do what he's craved for years. I've never been fond of the man, and after what I saw today, I don't think we can trust him. He's too unpredictable."

"I agree. After I am finished speaking to the group, I plan on making a trip back to the jail. I imagine some solitary time for those boys in green softened their hearts a bit. We'll just take Curt with us and lock him up until he comes down a few notches from his high horse. Reed, how many troops did you say were at the school?"

"Thirty. Got them locked up in the garbage area on the backside of the kitchen. One's injured.

Turner Addison put a bullet through his shoulder after Curt went all Rambo. It was chaotic."

"Can't say I'm surprised. We really can't expect people to act normal under these trying circumstances." Regina glances behind her and takes a deep breath. "Kyle, are the phones and internet still out?"

"Yep. Radios seem to be on the fritz, too. I sent Bailey and Allsop up to the roof to keep an eye out for more munchers. And troops. The way I figure it, once the remainder of the soldiers show up to the school and find their buddies locked up like animals, they'll be heading here with a big chip on their shoulders."

Wishing she didn't need to ask; she braces herself for the answer. "What did you do with the bodies inside the store?"

Reed put a warm hand on her shoulder. "Don't worry. We were gentle with them. They're out back in a refrigerated trailer. We'll give them a proper burial once we get a better handle on things."

"My, but aren't you two bundles of sunshine?" Regina jokes while smoothing out the wrinkles in the new sweater Kyle brought her to replace the bloodied shirt. "Okay, let's get this over with. Telling everyone the world is in a state of chaos should be fun. Not."

Jane veers left as Reed, Kyle, and Regina make their way to the bedding department. The large group quieted down somewhat after their initial chattering upon arrival. The areas in between the aisles are devoid of the usual displays, allowing the residents space to sit or stand. Regina stops at the edge of the throng of people and climbs up to the top shelf so they can all hear her speech.

Clearing her throat to get their attention, she waits until the noise from private conversations ends. The enormity of addressing so many people—something she never likes doing—coupled with the gravity of the situation, weighs heavy on her heart. Staring out at the pale, frightened faces of men, women, and young adults, all looking to her to say something to calm their fears, makes her feel inadequate and small and sick to her stomach. She forces the wave of dizziness threatening to overtake her vision back, refusing to let her own fears control her words.

"For those of you who don't know me, I'm Regina Parker, Chief of Police in Rockport. I have quite a bit to go over with you, so I'm asking you in advance to wait with all questions or comments you have until I finish."

Pausing to ensure their full cooperation, she stares out into too many sets of eyes to count, takes a deep breath, and forces her voice to sound authoritative, hoping to hide her own fears. "There's no easy way to say this, and I'm afraid we don't have the luxury of extra time for me to dance lightly around the subject, so forgive me for being blunt. We're in trouble. Not just as a community, a state, or even the country. This scourge has hit the entire globe, according to the email I received early this morning from Governor Strickland. At the time of the last communication, no one knew the cause of what's killing our friends, neighbors, and family members.

"What we do know isn't pretty. Cell phones, land lines, and the internet are no longer functioning. Before contact with those in higher authority was lost, it was related to us the Pentagon, D.C., and the White House are all down. President Thompson declared Martial Law. Travelling across state lines is barred. Y'all already know the National Guard was sent in to test each of you for signs of contamination. What you don't know, and God almighty I wish I didn't have to tell you, is the disease has spread at a phenomenal rate. Once infected, the transition rate happens within an hour."

The collective gasp from the crowd makes her own hair stand on end. *I know how each of you feel. Twilight Zone shit.*

"From observation, we have discovered those who've turned are attracted to noise, bright lights, the smell of blood, and flesh. They also will..." She pauses while swallowing the disgust rising from her chest, recalling the conversation she had earlier with Walt Addison, "...attack and eat each other if one is killed near them. They are fast and strong, and the only way we've seen to stop one is to destroy the brain, whether by bullet or blunt force trauma."

A woman from the back of the crowd gasps, followed by, "Oh, Lord, help us!"

"At this time, we still don't know all the particulars about what's killing people. It could be some sort of mutated virus, bacteria, or even fungal. Not enough information has been gathered to give you a list of all the symptoms of infection to look for, other than profuse sweating, a fever, and agitation. The military destroyed the remaining test kits at the school so we will need to rely upon our own observations. We have three nurses on hand so if you feel sick, please notify me immediately."

She pauses to catch her breath and steady her nerves.

"We didn't bring y'all here for any other reason except to protect you from being terminated by the government. Until we can get a better handle on things and fully understand the depth and breadth of this situation, y'all are welcome to remain here under our protection. However, if any of you desire to return home, or leave the county completely, y'all are free to do so. Remember, though, if you do leave and attempt to cross state lines, the chances of being stopped and interrogated, possibly taken into custody and even killed, are high."

Quiet whispers ripple through the crowd. She holds up her hands to silence them.

"Please, wait until I'm finished so everyone can hear me. We don't have time for me to repeat things. While we hunker down and gather ourselves back together, please remember a few things. One: we may be in the middle of a store stocked with water, food, toiletries, and medicine, but it won't last long if we don't ration carefully. There is no way to judge how long it will be before regular shipments start arriving again to restock."

Several heads bob in agreement.

"Two: the same goes for ammunition. There is only so much here, and it must be used sparingly. Three: please be mindful we are using items that aren't ours, nor that we've paid for. Treat your stay here as though at a relative's house. Clean up after yourselves and be mindful of the person next to you. We are all in this together. Most of you have seen what this sickness does—and how fast it happens when someone is infected. We can't let our guard down. We must remain vigilant while keeping our fears in check."

Someone yells, "Amen!"

"I know all of you are scared. I am too. What we are experiencing is unchartered territory. If we succumb to the fear this nightmare has brought, then we've already lost the battle. Now isn't the time to be divided. Now is the time to pull together as a community, presenting ourselves as a unified group. Help our friends, neighbors, and family members get through this and survive until the situation is contained. It's time to put aside our differences, old prejudices, ancient grudges, and work toward a common goal, which is to continue living in a world currently turned upside down."

A rumble of questions rises from the crowd. Regina struggles to catch a full sentence from anyone since all of them are yelling. The frenzy is interrupted by Bailey and Allsop running down the aisle, arms waving wildly, faces pale and full of terror.

"We've got a lot of trouble coming this way from the freeway!" Bailey yells after stopping directly below Regina's perch on the shelf. "I'm talking *hundreds* of the dead."

Several people gasp and a few women start crying.

Jesus, when will this end?

"That ain't our only problem." Allsop adds, clearly scared. "Troops are heading this way from the school. They ain't shooting at the dead, so I'm guessing they're only interested in us."

Regina yells over the noise, her own heart pounding with terror. "Those of you able to use a firearm, get to sporting goods right now. The rest of you form a protective circle around the children in the toy section. It's time to defend ourselves from the dead, and those who want us that way. Remember—the dead are to take shots only to the brain. Do your best to avoid injuring the living. Do not fire at the troops—and I mean it—unless I give the order."

Chapter 11 - Dangerous Roads

Saturday, December 20th – 1:10 p.m. – Mountain Standard Time

ROBERTO SANCHEZ RUNS his shaking fingers through the pile of damp hair on his head. The power has been out for over six hours, and even though he is in the basement of his house, the heat is oppressive. The fact that he is drunk and can barely stand doesn't help matters, either.

He's tried for hours to reach Benito on his cell phone after the first call yet hasn't been able to connect with him again. Teresa finally collapsed from the stressors of the missing Maria, coupled with the unbelievable events happening in Arizona. Though he loves Teresa—as much as he is capable of the emotion—he is glad she is out cold. Too many hours of listening to her cry and whine about the whereabouts of her sister grated on his last nerve. He tried acting concerned and hiding the fact he knew exactly what happened to Maria before he left for his bachelor party. Though he didn't agree with Benito using the girl as a sacrificial mule, he feared the man enough to keep his opinions to himself.

When the dead started walking around, Teresa's terror went into high gear—and so did Roberto's. Even though she didn't know the intimate details of Benito's involvement, Teresa had completely flipped out. She ran around the house like a crazy woman, going in circles several times. When the news reported what was happening and Teresa saw the disturbing images, her connection with sanity— which was already strained from the disappearance of Maria—severed. Between heavy bouts of crying, she grumbled about Maria and how she'd worked so hard planning the wedding for nothing.

Teresa is a stupid, stupid woman. Those trivial things no longer matter. Just one look outside and the mind goes into survival mode.

Glancing over at Teresa's sleeping frame less than twenty feet away, he grimaces, wishing he could do the same. Then again, if he does manage to shut his eyes and rest, will the dreams be worse than reality?

"No way. Nothing can be worse than this. I'm living in a nightmare— while wide awake."

Even though he mumbled them under his breath, Teresa stirs at the words. He doesn't move, praying she remains asleep. He is stressed beyond belief, and if she wakes up and starts whining again, he fears his reaction will be violent.

He waits several minutes until satisfied she is still out, pacing in wobbly circles. He needs to punch something—or someone—to get rid of the seething fury burning inside his mind. The fifth of tequila he's already drank hasn't helped wash away the insanity of what is going on outside of his house, nor did it help erase the images of the two bodies upstairs he killed.

Again.

He doesn't know how or why, but Benito and his stupid schemes are at fault for what is happening around the world. For the first time in years, he wishes the distance between Arizona and El Salvador wasn't so far. If he were closer, he'd leave the safe confines of his home, find Benito, and then beat the fool to death.

How could Benito have unleashed such a plague on the world? Didn't he pay attention to what his scientists concocted? Hadn't the formula undergone testing to ensure it worked before being distributed? The stuff was supposed to be addictive, not deadly.

A disturbing thought hits him right in the gut as though punched by an invisible hand: What if Benito did this on purpose?

His stomach sours at the insane thought. Benito is a damaged, vicious man, and Roberto knows about the horrible things he endured for years from Mario. Hell, everyone except Teresa and Maria knew the late Mario Alvarado was nothing more than a lowlife pedophile. Though he had no evidence to support his belief, he would wager all his assets that Benito had been the one who killed the old bastard and framed another. Over the years, Roberto kept this thought to himself, thinking Mario reaped the dirty seeds he'd sown, and Benito was justified in seeking revenge against the sick fucker.

He assumed after Benito took over the reins he would eventually get past the years of abuse; move on and enjoy the treasures he stole from the old geezer. In some ways, Benito did—like boning the man's youngest daughter. However, when Benito discovered Mario's secret hidden in the safe, the street trash from San Salvadore morphed into an obsessed man driven by his own insecurities and insatiable desire to have his name whispered in awed, hushed tones by other drug dealers around the world.

Unwilling to think about the disturbed man any longer, Roberto shifts mental gears, recalling when Carlos, Santos, and Gregory didn't answer his calls or return to his bachelor party.

When the trio didn't return, he realized there was a problem and naively assumed something went awry with the plans set out for Maria. Since the partygoers were drunk and high, they never noticed when he snuck out the back door of the strip club.

When he drove up and went inside the old slaughterhouse to see what was keeping them, he opened the door and discovered the unthinkable. Three dead men missing most of their flesh rambled around the inside of the building, biting, snarling, and tearing chunks of flesh from each other. Roberto's legs carried him just fast enough to outrun the bloodied, growling shells of Gregory, Santos, and Carlos, and back to his SUV.

In the rearview mirror, he watched in horror as the trio lurched off toward downtown Phoenix, leaving a trail of blood and gore in their wake.

By the time he made it back to the party, he was shaking so hard all he could think about was downing enough tequila to wipe away the images, het the second he entered the strip club, what he witnessed at the slaughterhouse was mild compared to what had happened inside while he was gone.

The scene was nothing short of a bloodbath, way worse than any horror movie set ever conceived. Roberto was no stranger to seeing death up close and personal, but nothing compared to the carnage in front of him.

Before leaving the party, he noticed two of his henchmen, Rico and Calvin, break out a huge pile of coke onto the table. Several of the strippers and other patrons swarmed the private room, each taking turns snorting up the white powder. Before it was all gone, Roberto stepped over and yanked the half-empty kilo from Rico, pocketing the blow for later.

Rico had arrived only a few hours prior from picking up a kilo from one of Benito's runners at the Mexican border. Though tempting and hard to resist taking a hit before he departed, Roberto left, assuming the party would still be rocking when he returned. The guests were so wasted they'd never notice him slip back inside.

He was wrong.

Dead, wrong.

While the music thumped and the strobe lights flashed in time with the beat, Roberto stood frozen at the front entrance, overwhelmed by all the blood coating the stage and leaking from the torsos of two strippers ripped into pieces. Rico—or what sort of resembled Rico—shoveled handfuls of intestines into his mouth.

Tables were flipped on their sides, chairs strewn across the dance floor. Not one bottle of booze behind the bar remained intact. Red dripped from the walls, the painted ceiling, and off the fake chandeliers. Chunks of muscle, skin, intestines, and other body parts littered the floor like putrid confetti, mixed with blood and liquor.

Calvin was about fifteen feet away to his right, the fingers of his left hand clutching a section of lower bowel, his nose and upper lip still coated in white powder. When he shot his right arm forward and ripped out another long string of intestine from what used to be Holly-Woody, the buxom brunette and star attraction of the biggest strip club in town, Pussy Pussy Bang Bang, Roberto puked. The stream of vomit continued to spew forth while Roberto backed out of the club, tripping and falling twice while running back to the SUV.

By the time he made it inside the vehicle, the retching stopped long enough for him to start the engine. In a panicked rush, he didn't notice the stream of people on the sidewalk up and down University Road. When he threw the vehicle into reverse, he ran over a few.

And then the screaming started, which brought out the former, beyond-recognition-partygoers of Pussy Pussy Bang Bang.

That's when the *real* screaming started.

At the time, Roberto still hadn't made the connection between the coke and the dead. That changed when he arrived home. He ran inside, clothes still covered in vomit, and went straight toward the enormous bar in the den.

The two men left behind to guard Teresa, Geraldo and Eduardo, followed him as he ran through the house.

Geraldo peppered him with a barrage of questions which were ignored. After downing several shots to stop his hands from shaking, he finally told the men about the night's previous events. Eduardo mocked him, asking what type of hallucinogen he was on. In a fit of anger, Roberto stormed back out to his vehicle and extracted the blow from underneath the passenger seat. He threw the package at Eduardo while yelling he wasn't on a damned thing.

Roberto had pointed to the dented bumper and blood stains on the back of the SUV. "Solid proof for you fools."

"Let's turn on the news, see what's going on," Geraldo had suggested as they walked back inside.

For the next half-hour, the three men sat hunched on the couch, flipping channels. Geraldo and Eduardo took several snorts to wake up, but Roberto decided to stick with tequila. A stimulant would just heighten his ability to remember what happened at the club and slaughterhouse. Alcohol was a great, temporary memory eraser.

Those thirty minutes on the couch, watching reports and videos flood the screen with the same type of awful things he'd witnessed earlier, were Geraldo and Eduardo's last moments alive.

After seeing similar events occur around the globe, he had retrieved his favorite handgun from the desk. No sooner had he locked and loaded a full magazine, than the den filled with strange, gurgling noises. He turned around and came face-to-face with what used to be Geraldo.

Without hesitating, Roberto blew the man's head off, trained the gun on Eduardo, and did the same.

It was at that precise moment he knew exactly what was going on—and how people were turning into bloodthirsty, flesh-eating monsters. He yanked out his other cell and called Benito to warn him. The connection was horrible, and Roberto barely got three sentences out before the line went dead. He redialed three times, yet Benito never answered.

Teresa flew down the stairs at the sounds of gunfire. Roberto had shut the door to the den and ushered her into the living room. He made the mistake of turning on the television to distract her from all the questions about the noise, and he'd regretted the decision. When she saw what was going on she lost it.

After the television switched over to the EBS system, the phones went dead and the internet was unavailable, Roberto made the mistake of going outside. Though they lived in an exclusive, upscale neighborhood, the location didn't matter. He spotted several lumbering bodies walking up and down the street, a few crouched in the middle of the road near their driveways, chewing on the flesh of those who hadn't turned.

He'd grabbed another bottle of tequila and yanked a screaming Teresa behind him, retreating to the basement, and they'd remained there for the last twenty-four hours. When the emergency sirens blared, followed by an order from some government fool for every citizen to present themselves for testing at their local high school, Roberto and Teresa cowered in silence.

He sighs while looking over at the remains of the laptop he'd destroyed earlier after the internet went down. The shattered remnants sit in silence next to a useless cell phone. For the first time in years, he wishes he had a land line, though he assumes telephone lines are down as well. The terrifying sounds from outside—the wails of victims running away in vain from their pursuers—the steady *bam bam bam* of gunshots and explosives, have driven him to the breaking point.

Daylight streams in through the small windows, so he creeps over and peers outside. A multitude of military vehicles swarm the streets, the soldiers in camo gunning down the things ambling around the neighborhood. Like swat teams moving in on a target, a band of them goes from house-to-house, kicking in the doors and storming inside. More gunfire erupts before the group exits without any civilians in tow. Smoke from numerous fires blocks out the clouds, and the beautiful, well-maintained street looked like a warzone. Abandoned vehicles line the curbs, some left with doors wide and engines idling. The continuous noise of people screaming for help sends waves of hysteria throughout his body.

He cannot stand another minute caged like an animal at a kill shelter, cowering in fear for his number to be called.

I've got to get out of here before they come in and kill me, but where will I go? Oh, shit, like it matters. I just need to stay one step ahead of those armed fools.

Looking over at Teresa, he feels nothing for the woman whom he's shared a bed with for years—at least not enough to wake her up. Squaring his shoulders, he nods his head once, the choice is made. Teresa will just slow him down, and the thought of trying to escape with a frantic woman by his side makes his head spin.

Engagement's over, mi cielo. Good luck. Maybe you'll still be asleep when they bust in and shoot you. Go, join your sister on the other side.

Ignoring Teresa, he speeds up the stairs and into the den. Upon opening the door, the stench of the two rotting corpses overwhelms him. Burying his nose in the crook of his arm, he dodges the bodies and heads straight to the wall safe, removes several stacks of cash, two more guns and magazines, his citizenship papers, and the keys to a tricked-out Jeep locked inside the garage.

Sweat pours from his face and neck while shoving all the items into a trash bin underneath the desk. His eyes water from the odor of the dead bodies less than fifteen feet away. Grabbing the container, he runs from the den and out the side kitchen door to the garage.

The sounds of the army outside draw closer. He tries opening the garage door with the automatic opener after starting the Jeep, but nothing happens.

"Shit! Forgot the power's out! Gotta lay off the booze for a while."

Jumping out of the Jeep, he dashes over to the metal door and pushes it up, giving a quick scan of the yard, thankful no hungry corpses or troops are in his driveway.

His excitement is short-lived.

The second he backs out of the garage a barrage of bullets spray the hood of the Jeep. One destroys the windshield, sending shards of sharp glass inside the interior, peppering his face and chest.

"Ha! You missed, assholes!"

Throwing the vehicle into drive, he drives through the manicured yard at full speed, noticing a Humvee barreling down on him in the rearview mirror. He exerts additional pressure on the accelerator.

He reaches the end of the street and turns left toward the entrance to the interstate, screaming obscenities at the men trying to stop him.

Dodging stalled cars, trucks, roadblocks, and several dead people, he pushes the Jeep to her mechanical limit. The occasional *ping* of a stray bullet hitting the vehicle causes him to grip the wheel harder. One blows out the back windshield and rips a hole in the passenger headrest.

"Missed again!" Roberto shouts, glancing over for a split second and eyeing the embedded bullet in the dashboard.

Taking his focus off the road is the biggest mistake Roberto Jesus Sanchez ever made.

"Oh, shit!"

Motor skills swimming in alcohol, he jerks the wheel hard right, trying to avoid a large group of dead people in the middle of the road, but fear causes him to overcompensate, and when the tires hit a pothole, the Jeep flips.

Without his seatbelt on, he bounces around like a child's doll, losing count of how many times his head and body slam against a hard surface. The sting of glass and debris pierces his skin in countless places. The Jeep rolls several times before coming to a halt on its side.

Stunned, blood pouring from his head and equilibrium off, he tries to move, but every inch of his body screams in pain. Upside down in the back seat, pinned beneath the crumpled roof, he has no choice except to beg for help from the people shooting at him seconds before.

He never gets the chance to utter one plea for assistance because several sets of cold, clammy hands reach through the busted windows of the Jeep and tear him to shreds before his brain has a chance to register the pain.

Chapter 12 - Payback

Saturday, December 20th – 2:20 p.m.

LIEUTENANT GERALD PACK cracks a wide grin as the parking lot of the supercenter came into view. Less than two klicks away, he is antsy to get things rolling. He double-checks his rifle, giddy as the familiar rush of the anticipation of a fight floods his system. Nerves on high alert ever since the phone call activating his unit nearly ten hours prior, he's been running on pure adrenaline.

He has never deviated from any directive given in all the years he's served his country. Today, during global chaos, he refuses to let the fear of the world collapsing stop him, either.

The orders are simple: terminate all untested citizens. He is a trained warrior and had been taught to bury his own personal feelings about instructions from his superiors, no matter how much he disagrees with them. Fortunately, he is right there with the brass on his current mission. If the world stands any chance of surviving the outbreak turning people into lurching, blood-thirsty monsters, drastic measures need to be taken.

It is simply a bonus he seeks retribution against those who killed and injured personnel under his care and locked up the remaining members of his battalion like wild dogs.

Though a slight time deviation of the plan happened because of the crazy, backwoods militia bastards, their stay of execution is almost over.

He is still riding the high from wiping out any possible infection from the citizens at the hospital. The few cops stationed there guarding the medical personnel from the dead let them right in. It took less than ten minutes to sweep the small hospital and remove all potential threats.

"Sir, how can you be sure the store is where they took them?" Private Richardson asks.

Gerald snorts while raising the binoculars to his eyes, scanning the area up ahead, noting every detail, including how many vehicles are in the parking lot. He spots two uniformed cops on the roof before they disappear down the hatch. "Richardson, you just confirmed what I've known for years."

"Excuse me, sir?"

"Anyone born after 1985 is dumber than a box of rocks. Seriously! Think, Private. Where else in this small town would they go? It's a bit cold to gather at the park."

Richardson's cheeks fill with pink from embarrassment. The boy clears his throat. "Uh, well, I—"

"That's why you're a grunt and I'm in charge. Jesus, your brain's been fried from too much sitting on your ass with your face buried in electronics! Let me spell it out for you. They weren't at the hospital or jail when we picked up the others, so the next logical gathering place for such a large group would be?"

"Walmart. Got it. Smart thinking, sir."

"Watch and learn, boy. When hunting prey, you must not think like a predator. You must slip into the weaker mind of your quarry and *think* like they would. Those fools believe they are safe inside the brick-and-mortar monument to capitalism. This is going to be easier than back at the school."

"You bet." Davenport adds. "Taking them all out at once is much simpler and certainly less time consuming than a handful at a time. Just one request, sir?"

Gerald already knows what the request will be, so he turns and faces Davenport in the backseat, gaze landing on the bandaged wound to the boy's shoulder. "If the little panty-wastes have the balls to come outside, or survive our initial attack, they're all yours. Promise. I've got my target set in my sights. He's going to wish he broke my neck rather than my nose."

"Appreciate that, sir." Davenport nods once. "I'll make sure they regret killing Martina and shooting me."

"Sir, we've got a problem up ahead." Richardson mutters.

Gerald turns back to the front, noting the fear in Richardson's voice, which pisses him off to no end. "Ignore them, boy, and stop sounding like a whiny female. Drive. They'll follow the noise of our vehicles just like the rest of the lurchers from the jail."

"Exactly, which is why I thought we should—"

"Private! Grow a pair, will you? I want them to follow us. Use your brain, fool. There's no telling how many armed rednecks are waiting for us inside the store. We know for sure two hundred. They could've picked up more on their ridiculous quest to save people who'll be dead soon. They'll have plenty of guns and ammunition, considering where they chose to hide. We need extra distractions. They'll focus on killing those lurchers, not us. Perfect cover."

Richardson's face blanches while gripping the steering wheel so hard his fingers turn bone white. Gerald refuses to look at the wimp any longer and motions for him to stop. Rolling the window down, he waves to the six Humvees behind them. In seconds, the vehicles all stop, forming a tight group consisting of the remaining members of the 1st Battalion.

He leans out the window. "Can't ask for a better escort, boys and girls! Standard takedown format, two-by-two. We'll make a lap of the location first, making sure the lurchers surround the place. Bennett, you got the rocket launcher prepped and hot?"

Corporal Gary Bennett is behind the wheel of the closest Humvee. He gives him a thumbs up. "Yes, sir, as requested. May I speak freely, sir?"

Bennett is about to challenge his authority, as he's done in the past. A wave of fury burned in

Gerald's stomach. "No. We've got our orders, and it is time to implement them."

"Sir, can't we just return to the base as ordered?" Richardson pleads. "There's no need for this. They won't make it long anyway."

Sweat bursts from his skin and drips down his forehead onto his stained jacket. Pulling out a field knife, he holds it up so Richardson can catch a glimpse of his little visual aide.

"Me and my friend Millie here are in charge now. If you want to try and challenge that, speak to her first. I guarantee you it will be a one-sided conversation—and one you won't enjoy. Those redneck fuckers locked you up in *jail*, or don't you remember that? Left you to slowly starve to death— or worse, had those lurchers made it inside—before we rescued you. Took your guns and left you sitting in the wind with your ass cheeks hanging out. Pick your side, Richardson, right now. Remember who freed you, and who left you behind bars."

"I can't do this. It's wrong. Not again. The hospital was bad enough. The memories of killing innocent civilians will haunt my dreams forever. I signed up with the Guard to help people. Please, sir, won't you reconsider? Isn't there any other any option?"

Gerald's touch with sanity snaps. Before Richardson utters another sound, he attacks. The blade is thick, sharp, and honed to perfection. With one swift stab, the cold steel penetrates the soft tissue at Richardson's temple, sliding in as easily as a hot knife through warm butter. When the hilt of the weapon reaches the boy's skull, he jerks the handle, scrambling the brains.

Pulling the blade free, he reaches over, unlocks the door, and kicks Richardson's limp body out of the front seat. Scooting over to take his place, he looks back out the window and over at Bennett. "Any of you other pussies want to express your opinions before we head out?"

No verbal responses, only blank stares of shock.

"Good. Time to move out. Follow my lead. Let's finish up our directive then head home. After what we've been through today, we deserve a bit of R&R."

Putting the Humvee in drive, he leads the way toward Walmart, not even trying to dodge the dead and dying littering the highway. Glancing in the rearview mirror, he notices some of the lurchers stopped, distracted by closer meat.

A few stragglers unwilling to join the party won't matter.

There are hundreds of others who will, and they are following the Humvees like flies drawn to rancid meat.

Chapter 13 - Defensive Maneuvers

Saturday, December 20th – 2:35 p.m.

WALT CROUCHES ON the roof, peering through the scope of the rifle. Turner is on his left, Martha on his right. Though the situation is dire, he takes comfort in the truth that at least he is surrounded by his family—in case this is the end. Less than five feet away are Curt, Bailey, Allsop, Newberry, and a few others, each fully armed. Footsteps crunch behind him and he knows they belong to tens of others who'd secured firearms and scrambled up to help. He gives them each a quick once-over, feeling the tension oozing from each as though living entities.

"I counted forty-two inside those six Humvees." Curt whispers after lowering the binoculars. "Damnation but I told you we should have taken their guns!"

"We ain't cold-blooded killers like you, Curt." Martha retorts. "But I guess that's gonna change here in a few minutes."

"Chief said not to shoot them unless she gives the order." Turner adds.

"Yeah, well she ain't here to stop me." Curt secures the binoculars before slinking down on his belly. He trains his rifle on the closest Humvee.

"Wrong." Reed's voice seethes with anger. "I'm here, and I swear Curt, if you fire one bullet in their direction, I'll take you out myself."

"So much for working together as a group." Turner shakes his head.

"Y'all need to remember which group poses the biggest threat!" Walt raises his voice to control the situation. "Those corpses out there can't be reasoned with. The live ones can. For Parker's sake, let's hope she knows what she's doing."

The rooftop falls silent. All eyes are focused on the horde of dead on the fringes of the parking lot. Another large group is closing in from downtown. There are too many to count, but he guesses around three hundred.

Studying the movements of the Humvees and the dead, he concludes the soldiers are using the corpses as a distraction. Just like Bailey and Allsop mentioned earlier, the troops don't seem interested in taking out the bodies. It looks like they are luring them to follow. "Jesus—those bastards are using the dead to distract us!"

Kyle rises and yanks a set of keys from his pocket. "You're right, Walt. Let's fuck up their plans."

"How?" Martha asks.

"Pull them away and get them to converge in one spot. It worked before." Kyle grins "They seem to love my unit. Hold your fire until the majority decide to check it out."

Kyle clicks the fob, and his patrol unit comes to life, blaring, beeping, sirens wailing, and lights flashing. Walt's eyes widen as the group at the edge of the parking lot turn their focus away from the Humvees and run toward Kyle's car. "Damn good idea."

"Steady. Wait until I give the signal." Kyle urges as his smile widens.

In seconds, his unit is no longer visible as the dead surround it, clawing, growling, gurgling at the noise.

The Humvees turn into the parking lot yet the undead don't seem to notice or care.

"Now!" Kyle yells.

A hail of bullets rains down from the rooftop. Heads explode and bodies crumple to the ground. Soon, the area around Kyle's car is covered in dark mahogany, the fallen bodies stacked almost three feet high. Their former neighbors, friends, and complete strangers went down in less than a minute.

Ears ringing from the noise, heart pounding from the excitement, and flashbacks of his time in the military, Walt blows out a burst of air after the last bullet fires. "Good job! That's one group down."

"Yeah, but the others behind the Humvees didn't take the bait." Reed points to the edge of the parking lot.

"Probably because most of them were grunts." Curt laughs. "They're dead yet still blindly following orders. Sacks of shit."

"Quit yapping like a bunch of proud hunters and get to reloading!" Martha urges. "Those Humvees only stopped while we were shooting."

While the group reloads, Walt's stomach remains in a tight knot. He knows what is coming next and thinks the Chief's plan is foolhardy and dangerous. Men like Lt. Pack cannot be reasoned with.

Period.

Of course, the stubborn woman wouldn't listen to reason, either. Not that Walt is surprised by Parker's attitude, for it is part of who she is and always will be, even during a shitstorm. When she gave her little speech, he fought hard to keep from cringing. Though he agreed with a good majority of the words, when she mentioned rationing supplies—and waiting for more to arrive—he almost laughed.

The woman is delusional if she thinks things will ever return to normal.

Thoughts about Parker's lofty ambitions vanish when he spots her frame in the parking lot.

And the Humvees inch forward.

She's toast. Damnit! They'll mow her down before she gets a chance to say one word.

"Hold your fire!" Reed shouts.

Walt's fingers shake. He grips the butt of the rifle, hoping Parker's daughter is still inside with the children.

He doesn't want the girl to watch her mother die in front of her eyes.

***

REGINA USES THE barrage of gunfire as her cue to slip out of the side door in automotive. While handing out guns, Kyle told her his plan to lure the dead to his unit. She knew it would work and sure enough, it did.

Rounding the corner by the garden center, she pauses, watching the six Humvees idle at the edge of the parking lot. Just as Allsop and Bailey stated, they aren't helping clear the area of the dead.

Instead, they sit and watch like spectators. Anger rumbles inside her chest. *How can they just sit there and do nothing? Said the fly to the spider.*

Bursting from her spot, she hugs the wall and runs to the main entrance. The blacktop glistens crimson, blood, and flesh cover Kyle's unit. Swallowing the disgust at the sight, she stops and faces the Humvees.

Once the shooting ends, the vehicles move forward. In groups of two, they scatter in different directions, a throng of the dead right behind them about one-hundred yards.

Two vehicles head straight toward her position. After saying a silent prayer, she holds up her hands. Summoning all her courage, she yells, "It doesn't have to end this way. Turn around and go back to your base. Leave us be."

Over the loudspeaker of the Humvee closest to her, a male voice responds, "We don't negotiate with terrorists."

The word choice infuriates her. "Terrorists? We're U.S. Citizens fighting to survive, and none of us are sick. We want to live, just like you."

"When someone takes out a soldier, it's terrorism. The penalty is death by firing squad."

The response confirms her suspicions—the lieutenant is on the loudspeaker. "Since when does an entire community owe a debt for the actions of just one citizen, Lt. Pack?"

"Since I'm in charge."

She takes a deep breath, hating herself for what she is about to say, yet there is no choice except to offer up the illusion she is willing to negotiate a trade. Her plan is to inch close enough she can take out the leader with one shot and the others will either scatter or at least give up. "If we hand him over to atone for his crime, will you agree to spare the rest of us?"

Silence.

The lead vehicle stops. An arm extends from the window instructing the others to do the same. The remaining five Humvees halt without making it far from their original position.

A sense of dread—her new constant companion—slithers around inside her chest. The dead are closing in behind the Humvees, and any second, someone on the roof will fire again and this time, the target will be living soldiers. She must hurry.

Forcing her muscles to obey, she walks toward the Humvee, arms still in the air, making it less than twenty feet before the voice she assumes is the lieutenant barks, "That's far enough."

Sweat covers her entire body. Though she wills them to stop, her muscles quake in response to the grumbling dead behind the vehicles. "I'll ask you again—leave us be. I'm Rockport's chief of police and take full responsibility for those inside."

"That's a risky choice to make Chief." Lt. Pack's tone is rude and snarky. "Any other time, I'd consider the offer, but not today."

The Humvee on the right shoots forward, spins around, and stops directly in front of the lieutenant's vehicle. A man in uniform jumps out from the driver's side, rifle pointed at the cab. "This isn't right, Pack. Let it go or I swear I'll shoot. I'm not gonna stand by and watch you kill these people."

What happens next is a complete blur. Lt. Pack explodes. "Traitor!"

And then, all hell breaks loose.

Hot, burning pain explodes in her thigh before her ears register the repeat of a rifle. The impact throws her onto the hard blacktop. Gunfire erupts all around, coming from every direction.

Adrenaline in overdrive, knowing another stray bullet will be her last, she reaches behind her back and grabs the handgun stuffed in the waistband. Rolling onto her stomach, she aims for the craniums of the dead. The soldier who stepped out of the Humvee fires numerous rounds into the windshield of Lt. Pack's vehicle. She hopes one of the bullets blew the lieutenant's head off.

The noise agitates the dead. No longer lumbering, they pick up their pace and in seconds, the parking lot is crawling with them. In the distance, the voices of Reed and others shouted for her to get up and run. In the back of her mind, fear whispers for her to heed the instructions, yet the heat of the moment overrides the fear, and she holds her position.

The soldiers inside the Humvees climb out onto the roofs of their vehicles, take aim, and fire at the onslaught of the dead, trying in vain to stop their push forward.

It doesn't work. They are grossly outnumbered.

In horror, she notices several undead climbing up to the roof tops.

Oh, God. They figured out how to climb?

The realization spurs her to stand, knowing only a few rounds remain in the magazine. She clamps down on her bottom lip, keeping the scream of agony inside while limping back toward automotive.

"Rocket launcher! Get down!" someone screams.

Regina freezes, gaze trained on Lt. Pack.

Time slows as her brain is bombarded with sensory overload.

Lt. Pack screams like a wild boar and lunges from the Humvee. Sunlight gleams off the long knife in his hand before it disappears inside the abdomen of the soldier in front of him. The man collapses and crawls to the underbelly of the nearest Humvee. Another grunt exits a different Humvee clutching a shoulder-held rocket launcher aimed at the store's entrance.

I can't let him fire that thing!

Calling upon every muscle to work, she shifts directions, stumbling forward until closing the gap between them. She only needs a few more feet before in range to shoot.

Another Humvee swerves into the parking lot then stops. A man jumps out, holding another launcher to his shoulder. Regina stops, plants her feet, gets a good sight picture, and fires at the one closest to her position, aiming for the bandaged wound on the man's shoulder.

She hits her target, but it doesn't matter.

The impact of the bullet causes the man's torso to shift right yet doesn't stop him from depressing the trigger. A loud *whoosh* followed by a trail of smoke and fire, blows from the mouth of the weapon. Rather than hitting the main entrance, the missile rips through the chain-link fencing surrounding lawn and garden.

The force of the blast knocks Regina backward. She feels her body soar through the air for what seems like hours.

God, please take care of my family.

It is the last thought in her mind before she slams into the ground.

***

Walt could not believe Curt stood and shot Parker. Without thinking of the consequences, he turns his weapon on him and blows a hole through the chest of a man he's known for over twenty years. "You're the traitor!".

There isn't time to say another word, or dwell on the fact he killed his friend, because over fifty people on the roof opened fire on the crowd in the parking lot.

From his periphery, he sees Reed turn and run. He knows the man isn't fleeing in fear to hide or save his ass—he's running in desperation to save his sister.

Returning all his attention to the scope, Walt takes in a huge gulp of cold air through his nose and lets it out in a slow, even stream through his lips. The action helps control the shakes, so he won't miss his targets. The dead drops in droves from the spray of bullets from his rifle and the others on the roof.

Another Humvee pulls into the parking lot at the exact moment Lt. Pack jumps from his perch inside the confines of the Humvee. In the blink of an eye, the cruel bastard guts one of his soldiers.

"Fucker! I'll get you!" Walt mutters to himself.

The movement of another behind the lieutenant catches his attention. He recognizes the shape, and seeing one transports him back years to the time in his life he's tried in vain to bury.

"Rocket launcher! Get down!"

He throws himself on top of Martha, covering her body with his, hoping to shield her from flying debris and shrapnel. The explosion shakes the entire building, drowning out the screams of those around him.

Closing his eyes, he whispers a silent prayer, fully aware any second will be their last after the building crumbles around them. To his surprise and relief, that doesn't happen, so he opens his eyes and looks around. Dust and debris hang in the air to his right. Rising enough to see over the edge, he's stunned. "I'll be damned! He missed us!"

"Another one has a launcher!" Turner yells.

Kyle raises his rifle to his shoulder and peers through the scope. "Got him—oh, shit! That's Shaun Kilpatrick! Wait, hold your fire. Look where he's aiming!"

"He's gonna take all of them dead out, including them malicious bastards in green!" Lamar pumps his fist in the air.

Walt scans the parking area, spotting Parker motionless on the ground about twenty feet away from where the rocket exploded. Two figures burst from the smoky, destroyed area, dodging smoldering chunks of debris while running to her side.

Turner must have noticed the same thing because he stands and yells, "Jesse, what are you doing? Get back inside. Hurry!"

An explosion from another missile launches three Humvees and countless bodies into the air. When they land, two vehicles burst into flames. Dark, thick smoke rolls into the sky, sending plumes of black thirty feet into the air.

"I'll be damned! He took out all those green bastards in one swoop." Turner looks impressed and scared.

Burnt body parts rain down on the parking lot. The sickening *plop plop plop* as each one lands makes his stomach roil.

"What the hell is that fool doing?" Lamar points.

"Getting himself killed." Kyle rises. "Shaun, don't! Run! Behind you!"

Walt grabs the binoculars resting next to Curt's dead body and sure enough, Shaun Kilpatrick runs straight into the melee, dives under a Humvee, and exits the other side with the soldier who'd been stabbed firmly in his grip.

"Get to automotive. Now!" Kyle instructs. "We've got to go back down, see what type of damage the missile did to lawn and garden and shore it up before those stunned munchers realize they have a way inside."

Kyle's words slap the group out of their shocked state. In minutes, the rooftop is empty after they dash back inside.

"Bailey, Allsop, Kyle, Lamar, Martha, and Turner: follow me to lawn and garden." Walt's voice is thick with emotion. "The rest of you form a line of defense around the residents inside. We'll assess the damage and fix whatever hole was created to keep those dead bastards outside."

The group breaks off and scatters upon reaching the main floor. People are crying and some scream from fear and pain.

Racing down the aisles, they make it to what is left of lawn and garden. Dust hangs in the air, bricks and various pieces of equipment litter the floor. His heart sinks after surveying the extensive damage.

The outer portion, including the chain link fence housing mowers, plant containers, and various types of lawn care items, is gone. The glass doors on the left leading out to the courtyard are no longer visible. All that remains is the metal housing they'd been encased in, which hangs in bent tatters. Despite the dust, he has a clear view into the parking lot.

The dead are less than two hundred feet away.

The place he's been hundreds of times to buy items for his own house looks like a warzone, barely recognizable from its previous state.

"The hole's too big and there's nothing left here to use to form some type of barrier." Martha eases next to him and touches his arm.

He takes a deep breath while locking gazes with his bride. Earlier, she'd looked scared yet determined. Now, she looks downright terrified, determination long gone.

"Mom's right. We need to get everyone outta here before those things notice the way in." Turner offers. "Maybe over to the hospital or jail?"

The heavy rock of worry sitting in Walt's stomach morphs into a boulder. "I say we head to our beta location."

"And leave all these people here to fend for themselves?" Martha gapes at him. "Are you crazy? Why did we just risk our lives to save them, only to turn tail and run?"

"We aren't gonna be safe here, Ms. Martha. Not for long." Lamar joins the discussion. "What choice do we have? I agree with Walt. Let's gather as much food and medicine as we can carry and get the hell outta here before Walmart becomes our final resting place."

Turner steps closer and stares at the parking lot. "They still seem sorta stunned. We need to make our choice before they snap outta their funk."

Martha grabs his arm and squeezes. "Walter— we can't just let the others stay here alone. Let's get them out back and into the vehicles. We'll head to the hospital. Needed to get there anyway, since Marian Kilpatrick is in labor."

Staring at the tufts of pink insulation hanging from the rafters, listening to the building creak and groan as chunks of ceiling tiles and plaster cascade onto the floor, he wipes sweat from his brow. The structure is heavily damaged, and he doubts it will remain standing for more than an hour.

Backing up, he signals to the others to do the same. "Whatever we decide, we need to do it fast. This place is a ticking time bomb."

"Help, please!"

All of them freeze at the sound of a man's voice from the outside.

"That's Shaun!" Kyle whispers.

"Damnit!" Walt turns and faces the remainder of the group. "Get back inside and start gathering supplies. I'll catch up. Get those trucks filled up. Have a feeling we're gonna need them soon."

The others leave and Walt creeps through the debris. He reaches the destroyed entrance, keeping in a groan of irritation. The soldier Lt. Pack tried to gut earlier sags in Shaun's arms.

Without a word, Walt grabs the man's feet and helps Shaun carry him back inside. Blood seeps from the abdominal wound, oozing through the soldier's clenched fingers.

He ain't gonna make it. Why are we even trying?

Chapter 14 - Descent into Madness

Saturday, December 20th – 3:15 p.m.

JESSE FORCES HERSELF to remain calm and not cry after reaching her mother's limp body on the blacktop. Blood soaks the ground around her, the front of her torso is covered in dirt and debris. Bending down, she grabs the gun resting near her mom's hand and secures it inside her waistband.

"Grab her legs. Easy now." Reed urges. "On the count of three."

In shock and unable to speak, she nods, latches onto her mother's feet, and bites her bottom lip to keep from sobbing out loud after her mother groans. *She's alive! Thank God! Momma, hang on. Don't die. Please? You can't leave me—I need you.*

"One, two, three!"

Pushing her body, calling upon strength she didn't think she possessed, she follows her uncle's instructions and helps hoist her mom from the ground. She ignores the sharp pain in her back while they jog back inside.

When less than five feet away from the smoldering hole in lawn and garden, another explosion rocks the ground, quaking underneath them. She nearly loses her grip on the slippery, wet material of her mom's pants, yet somehow manages to hang on.

"Head to where Marian and Jane are. We'll need plenty of cloth to stop the bleeding."

She nods at her uncle.

Stumbling over the chunks of the damaged building on the floor, she shut out the wails of others, the sound of gunfire, and the screams. They worm their way through the aisles, passing several people who've given up on Walmart being a haven and run to the back of the store, yelling advice to others to do the same.

"I've got room for three."

"Got an SUV that can fit eight. Come on, it ain't safe here no more!"

"I ain't dying here! Going home to get my dog and hunker down. Coming here was a huge mistake!"

A frazzled looking woman, one Jesse vaguely recognizes, runs up beside her, mounds of knotted red hair frame her face. "Tell your mom we appreciate what she did, but we aren't staying. We'll pray for her."

Had she been able to form words, it wouldn't have mattered because the harried woman turns and disappears into a throng of others scrambling to reach the back of the store, arms full of whatever they can carry.

She frowns at all thankless bastards rushing past.

Continuing forward, they round the corner to the aisle where Jane sits hunched next to Marian Kilpatrick. The woman makes the *hee-hee, hoo-hoo* sounds Jesse's heard on television by women in labor.

"Jane!" Reed shouts over the noise. "Need some help here."

"Wait, let me spread out something." Jane jumps to her feet and yanks off the plastic covering a thick comforter. With one swoop of her arms, numerous white pillows fall off the shelves. Jane moves quickly and pushes the pillows together before covering them with the frilly, pink comforter.

Jesse gawks at them, thinking the comforter looks just like the one on her bed at home. God, is she thinking about things that don't matter when her mother is dying right in her arms?

"Jesse, let's ease her down, nice and easy."

Uncle Reed's words pull her back to reality. She nods.

"What happened?" Jane asks.

"She took a round to the thigh, and then was too close to the explosion. It knocked her back about twenty feet."

The second her mom's head touches the pillow, she groans again and her eyes flutter open. Jesse's shattered mind struggles to maintain sanity. Removing the gun from her waistband, she sets it down and scoots over to the other side, stroking her mother's cold, blood-soaked hand. "It's okay, Mom. Jane's gonna fix you right up."

"Did we get 'em?"

"Yeah, we did, sis. All those military fools are gone."

Jesse smiles at her uncle before grabbing a pillowcase from the shelf and wipes away the stream of blood oozing from her mom's mouth. "Don't talk, Mom. Save your strength."

"Oh, God, another one's coming!" Marian whines.

A warm hand touches Jesse on her shoulder. "Honey, let me tend to your momma. I need to bandage her leg, and you don't need to see that, so go offer a hand for Martha to grip during her contractions."

"No. I'm not leaving Mom's side. I can help you patch her up."

"Do what she asks, Jesse. I'll be fine. It's okay, Marian, just remember to breathe. Ain't nothing more natural to a woman's body than giving birth."

"Not...like...this, *hee-hee, hoo-hoo*, and not now! Please...get...this...thing...outta me!"

Watching one woman struggle to bring life into the world while another clings to keep from dying, makes Jesse nauseous. All the chaos, the stomping of feet against the floors as people scramble about, the whimpering of children and screams of adults— it is too much. The overstimulation makes her vision blur and hands shake.

"Jesse—move. I must stop the bleeding."

Hearing the change in Jane's voice, Jesse moves over and holds out her hand to Marian. Something warm and wet coats her cheeks and it takes a few seconds for her brain to register the wetness is hot tears from watching the nurse work on her valiant mom.

"Reed, I need several things from the pharmacy. Hold this pillow right here and press down with all you've got. I'll be right back."

Jane rises and takes off, dodging panicked residents while making her way to the other side of the store. Jesse loses visual in seconds when the crowd swallows her up.

Looking back over at her mother, she stifles a gasp then turns away from the sight as Uncle Reed presses down on the pillow. Her mother yelps in agony and the sound sends chills up her spine. She's never seen her mother in any other light except as a tough, headstrong woman. The new, weaker side makes her heart clench in agony.

Her mother whispers something, but Jesse cannot make out what was because of the ridiculous racket coming from Marian. The woman's grip is strong enough to crush the bones together. She lets go before the stupid woman breaks her hand.

Marian leans back against the shelf, sweat pouring from a cherry-red face. "I can't do this. Can't deliver in the middle of all this! God, why now?"

"Yes, you can, Marian. You must. Your little one needs you."

"Mom? What's wrong with your voice? It sounds funny."

"Nothing. Just got the wind knocked outta my sails, that's all. Marian—what's your baby's name?"

It is just like her mother—ignoring her own discomfort and pain to help another.

"I don't want it." Marian whispers. "Not now. What if something happens to me? Who'll be left to take care of her?"

"Marian, stop it. Of course you want her. Nothing is more precious in this world, even this fucked up one, than a child. You'll never be more filled with love than the first time you set your eyes on her. That's a promise. Children are everything. They make all the pain of living worth it. Besides, you have Shaun to help you."

"Shaun ain't here, just like always. Too busy out playing in the woods with his stupid friends."

"Girl, you gotta learn that's how men get rid of their anxieties. Right, brother?"

"Regina's right, Marian. Hunting is just a male version of a hen party."

Marian waves her hand in the air. "Whatever. You two don't know Shaun. He doesn't love me. We're only getting back together because of this monster in my...oh, shit! Another one!"

Jesse flinches as Marian latches onto her hand.

"Reed? Need a place to put him."

Ignoring the pressure crushing her bones together, Jesse looks up. At the end of the aisle is Turner's dad, along with Shaun Kilpatrick. In between them they hold the limp body of a soldier covered in bright, red blood.

"Sorry, can't let go." Reed shakes his head.

"I've got it." Jane yells from behind them.

In seconds, the men deposit the man next to Jesse. The aisle way is covered in the blood of her mother and the man. Jane bends down next to him, performing a quick assessment. From the look on her face things are bad.

"He needs surgery right now to stop the internal bleeding, and I mean immediately."

"Then let's get him to the hospital." Shaun offers. "I've got keys to a Humvee."

"Shaun!" Marian yells while letting go of Jesse's hand. "Oh, Shaun…our baby…she's coming."

She trades places with him. He squats down next to his wife, removes the strap of his weapon from around his neck, he sets it down near Jesse and grabs Marian's hand.

"It's okay, sweetie. We'll take you, too. Right?" Shaun looks over at Walter for confirmation.

"We can fit them both in the backseat." Walt nods. "Plenty of room in that gas-guzzler."

"Good!" Regina smiles. "Marian, you and I can ride together. See? It's gonna be okay. Your little one can wait a few more minutes. We'll make the trip together."

"Regina? You need to stop talking. Right now." Jane instructs, voice clipped and harsh. "Jesse? Come over here and hold pressure. Reed, I need to speak with you and Walt."

"What? Why?" Jesse asks.

"Do it!" Jane's tone is full of fear.

Jesse jumps into action, swapping places with her uncle and forcing herself not to gag as her fingers press down on the bloodied material. Unwilling to look at the oozing red from the wound, she focuses her gaze on her mother.

"It's okay, honey. Let them talk." Regina whispers.

Nodding in agreement, Jesse watches the trio move to the end of the aisle, Jane's lips moving a mile a minute.

What the hell is going on?

***

"He's not going to make it, even if he was on the operating table with a skilled surgeon working on him." Jane's voice is a low whisper. "I give him five minutes—tops. All we can do for him now is make sure he's comfortable, and not let him die alone."

"That's a no-brainer." Walt sighs. "Knew it the minute I laid eyes on him. People usually don't survive being gutted."

Reed's stomach drops. He knows from the tone in Jane's voice the life span of the soldier isn't why she'd pulled them away from the others. "It's Regina, isn't it?"

Jane nods, the look of anguish on her face makes his chest tighten.

"Yes. That wheezing in her voice that sounds like she's talking with water inside her throat is because her lungs are punctured and filling with blood and bodily fluids. I went back to the pharmacy to look for something to open her up with and use as a drain, but there wasn't anything usable. People already picked it clean."

Reed closes his eyes, heart pounding in his chest. He nods for Jane to continue, wishing he was at home, in bed, and could awaken from the worst nightmare he's ever experienced.

"She's got several broken ribs on each side. However, the mortal injury is from the gunshot. The bullet tore through her femoral artery. The moment we let off the pressure, she'll bleed out in seconds. How she made it this far is simply a miracle."

"Jesus. This isn't happening." Reed shoves his trembling hands into his pocket in case Jesse is watching. "I knew Curt was unstable. We should've hog-tied his ass before he had a chance to shoot her. Stupid fool. He had no idea what she was planning!"

"Take some comfort in the fact he won't ever hurt another." Walt adds.

Shifting his weight, unable to stand still, he locks gazes with Jane, fighting to keep the tears at bay and his voice from cracking. "Why are we standing here discussing this? Shouldn't we take her to the hospital? At least it will give her a chance?"

Jane puts a warm, comforting hand on his arm. "It won't. The reason she's so sweaty and pale is because, in my opinion, she's at least in Stage 3, if not Stage 4, of hypovolemic shock. Regina's simply lost too much blood, internally and externally. I've seen this hundreds of times over the years from traffic accident victims."

"Since we're dropping bombs of good news here, let me add another. The missile did some major damage in terms of our security. There's a gaping hole with no way to seal it in lawn and garden. Even though Shaun swooped in and took out all those grunts and quite a few of the dead, we didn't get them all. Once they realize there's a way inside here, this place will turn into one giant smorgasbord, with us as the main course."

Reed gapes at Walter. "Are you suggesting we just leave the injured behind and run away like cowards?"

"Of course not. What kind of monster do you think I am, Newberry? No, I'm suggesting we extract ourselves from this breached haven and get *all* of us to the hospital. If the grunt who tried to help us outside and Regina aren't going to make it, we can at least sleep tonight knowing we tried until the very end. At least we'll get that pregnant lady to the right place to deliver a baby."

"Jesse's going to..." Reed cannot bring himself to finish the sentence.

"Look, here's the deal. My wife, son, Lamar, Kyle, and others are loading up supplies as we speak. They know, because we already discussed this after viewing the remains of the garden center, the next step is to head to the hospital. Half of those we brought here earlier already left, and I hate to say it, but maybe them leaving will distract the dead still lurking outside long enough for us to get out safely."

"Then it's settled. Let's stop wasting time and get them out of here."

Gunfire erupts from the end of the aisle, drowning out the rest of Reed's response. Spinning around, his breath catches in his throat when the dead descend on groups of people across the store.

Several close in on Regina with Jesse about six feet away. To his surprise, his niece fires into the throng, missing more than connecting.

Regina screams, "Jesse! Shaun! Run, now!"

His heart shatters. *Oh, my God. We're too late.*

***

REGINA KNOWS SHE only has minutes, if not seconds, left to live. She can feel her strength diminish with each faint heartbeat and every intake of air is torture, sending white-hot pain rippling throughout her body.

She must maintain a strong face for Jesse. The words she'd said earlier to Marian probably haven't soaked through the haze of hysteria in Jesse's mind yet, but one day, they will. Her daughter will smile when remembering the sneaky way she conveyed her love through the conversation.

Regina wasn't afraid of dying like she'd always assumed she would be. A strange sense of peace and warmth floods her mind, and she wonders if that is due to lack of blood or simply coming to terms with the truth that her time to join her husband on the other side awaits.

"Mom? Mom?"

Licking dry lips, she struggles to open her eyes, which she hadn't realized are closed.

"Just…resting my eyes, baby."

"No, you weren't. You passed out. Please, Momma, stay awake. We need you. I need you."

From the corner of her eye, she notices Shaun stand and head toward the others at the end of the aisle. Marian takes a deep breath and shifts her position on the floor. Blinking twice, Regina focuses her gaze on her daughter's worried face. Her baby girl, still dressed in pajamas yet finally with a coat on, hair sticking up in every direction, looks like a harried angel. "Have I told you how much I admire you?"

A few tears slide down Jesse's face. "Admire me? What in the world for? I've done nothing but cause you grief."

"Wrong. You're stronger than you know; tougher than me. You kicked a habit that usually kills most; beat the devil at his wicked game. That's strength. That's heart. That's what makes you special. Heart."

Jesse dabs her sleeve on Regina's mouth, swiping dribbles of blood away. "Stop that, Mom."

"Stop what?"

"Talking like you're dying. I won't listen."

She winces while taking another breath. "I am, and you will listen to me for Turner and for your uncle. The world's gonna need strong women to help rebuild it. Now's your time to shine."

"Horseshit! You're not dying. I won't...I won't let you!"

"Everyone has an expiration date, daughter. Everyone. Make the most of the allotted time. Be honest. Stay true to what I've taught you. Do what your heart knows is right. Take care of Turner. He loves you more than you know. Reminds me a lot of your dad."

"You taught me to never give up, and that's exactly what I'm doing!" Jesse bursts into tears.

"Listen to your own preachings, Mom. You're giving up on yourself."

She coughs, and the pain tries to pull her into black oblivion, but she hangs onto the light surrounding her daughter's face. "Coming to terms with the inevitable ain't giving up, darling. It's called acceptance."

"Please, don't leave us." Marian whimpers.

Regina turns her head, noticing the woman is now closer. She forces a smile to appear. "You take care of your little one, Marian."

"I won't listen to any more of your bullshit, Mom. Oh…my…God!"

Jesse's defiant words stick in her throat as her eyes go wide, fear causing her face to turn stark white. Before Regina has a chance to ask what is wrong, Jesse lets go and scrambles across the floor, retrieving Shaun's rifle.

Regina knows then what her only child is aiming at—and what sent her into a frenzy.

Summoning every ounce of strength, she reaches out and feels around for her pistol, praying Reed or Jesse brought it back with them. Touching the cold steel, she grabs it, trying to remember how many rounds she'd shot while in the parking lot.

It doesn't matter. You'll only need one.

Twisting her head to the right, her heart flutters.

Four monsters are closing in.

Fast.

Time slows to a crawl as she comes to grips with what she'll have to do to ensure her daughter and brother survive.

There is no way Reed, Walt, or Jane will make it to her and Jesse in time to rescue them both. She also knows her brother will try, which will just end up being the last thing he does before being ripped to shreds.

Regina Newberry Parker will not let that happen, not while she is still able to do something to change the outcome of a horrible situation.

She will serve.

Shaun is about seven feet from Jesse, who continues firing at the dead. She prays her baby girl inherited her marksmanship skills.

"Oh, Jesus! I don't want them to eat my baby. I can't stand up—another contraction's coming!" Marian screams.

Marian and Regina exchange glances and in that split second, both women know exactly what the other is thinking. Marian nods, tears running down her face while moving closer and resting her head underneath Regina's.

"Jesse! Shaun! Run, now!" Regina screams. The effort makes stars dance behind her eyes.

Reed and Walt are running full blast. They reach Jesse and Shaun close to the same time. Reed throws his arms around Jesse, dragging her, kicking, and screaming, backward, and Walt does the same with Shaun.

The sounds of Jesse and Shaun yelling to be released, the sporadic gunfire from other areas of the store, the screams of terrified people, all turn into background noise. The only sound she focuses on is the mewling, grumbling, growling of the dead closing in behind her.

I'm not going to miss that sound. Forgive me, Lord. Watch over them and please, let all of them make it out of here. Alive.

"Hurry." Marian groans as another contraction hits.

With tears streaming down her face, Regina clutches her left hand with Marian's, using the right to stick the barrel of the gun underneath the woman's chin.

She will protect.

Marian squeezes her hand.

Both of their bodies shake as the first cold, dead hands latches onto them, pulling flesh away.

With her last breath, unable to get her voice above a whisper, Regina instructs her loved ones to run before leaning forward, chin resting on top of Marian's head, and pulling the trigger.

Chapter 15 - Darkness Falls

Saturday, December 20th – 5:15 p.m.

EVERETT STARES AT HIS notes while his lips curve into a twisted grin. His handwriting is still atrocious and had been the source of many jokes by family and friends. Carol used to tease him, saying he was in the right profession.

His fingers ached from clutching the pen for so long. He set it aside and rubs the red, swollen knuckles, cursing his age under his breath, wishing he'd remembered to pack arthritis medication.

A dull, continuous throbbing in his temples feels like someone has their fingers pressed against his head all because he'd stared at the small print of the medical books spread out in front of him for too long. When younger, things such as reading or writing pages and pages of notes were simple, easy tasks, but age made them just as difficult as dropping down and banging out one-hundred sit-ups.

Back stiff from sitting in the same spot, he stands and stretches, desperate to get his blood pumping.

Porterfield and Warton left to get a specimen hours ago, and he needs to be ready to work when they return.

Leaving the lab, he walks down the quiet hallway. Though he spent ten years of his life inside the place, being at Dr. Thomas' residence for the better part of a year had spoiled him. Claustrophobia fights to overtake his thoughts, reminding him of the struggle the first two years he'd been underground.

"No, stop. You aren't down here alone. This place won't be your tomb. It's only temporary."

His mumbled words bounce off the concrete floors and walls, sending chills up his back in response to the strange way his voice echoes. He quickens his pace, hoping he'll run into Dirk or one of the other men before his fear of being alone drives him mad.

The door to the room where Susan, Diane, and all the other former addicts lost their lives is only feet away. His mouth fills with hot saliva. Being underground, in the bowels of a mountainside, is bad enough, but the knowledge so many people were murdered at one time, trapped inside a place most didn't come to willingly, makes him feel sick to his stomach.

If he believed in haunted places full of the restless ghosts of those unable to move on to the next plane of existence because of the tragic ways they'd departed, the windowless room would certainly fit the bill.

He stops at the door, refusing to go inside, and places a hand on the cool metal, saying a silent prayer for them while recalling the conversation with Dirk months ago after he finally convinced the man to tell him what happened inside the lab. He cringes at the memory. Cyanide poisoning is a horrible way to exit the world. When Dirk told him, he remembers wishing the lab would have blown up because the death experience of those poor souls would have been quicker and less painful.

He tries imagining Daryl Riverside walking into the room, all smiles and kind words, the mop of hair flopping in his face while he handed out lunch and drinks to the unsuspecting group. Did any of them sense something was wrong? Did one of them pick up any negative vibes? Did any of them smell the scent of almonds as they brought drinks to their noses?

Warm tears run down his cheeks as he continues offering prayers.

"Doc? Stop it."

"Dirk, didn't you know the second sign of dementia is random bouts of crying?" He removes his hand from the door and rakes it across his fac, wiping away the wetness.

"Bullshit. I know what you're doing—blaming yourself for something that was never in your control. Stop it."

"Say what you will, you won't change my mind. Their blood is on my hands. They died, along with Roberta and Jason, as a direct result of my actions or rather, inactions. I should have watched Daryl closer, but I was too consumed by my work to pay any attention to my surroundings and those working alongside me."

"Aren't you tired of singing the same martyr song? I'm certainly sick of hearing it."

"We are two very different people, Dirk. You've experienced all this before. I haven't, so forgive me for feeling sad."

Dirk furrows his brow. "Was that your way of saying I'm a cold-hearted bastard, unable to experience grief or sorrow? If so, you're wrong. Dead, wrong."

Unable to face the man any longer, he walks back toward the main lab. "I...no, that's not what I meant. See? I cannot even articulate my feelings without screwing up. What I wanted to convey was I'm unaccustomed to being a party to murder."

"Thanks for explaining. So, now I'm an emotional zombie and a killer. Nice."

"Who's the martyr now? Can we just forget you found me wallowing in sorrow like a lost goat, and my woefully inadequate ability to express my thoughts on the subject? I've got more studying to do before Porterfield and Warton return."

Dirk follows him inside the lab and walks over to the workstation where he left numerous medical books on the table.

Picking up *Essentials of Glycobiology* by Nizet and Esko, he frowns. "Glycan-binding receptors, initial colonization, epithelial surfaces? Is this even in English?"

Everett hopes the humorous comment is Dirk's way of showing he'd accepted the apology. He isn't completely sure as he's still learning how to read the former soldier. "As you mentioned earlier, I've got to man-up and figure out what's going on, right?

The best way to start, in my opinion, is to reacquaint myself with infectious diseases."

Dirk returns the heavy book to the table. "Good thing you're here, because if the world's survival depended upon us grunts, we'd be toast."

***

Kevin Warton lowers the binoculars and sighs.

"What is it?" Porterfield asks.

"Here. See for yourself." He hands the lenses over. "Words just won't do."

He glances down from their perch on the large set of boulders. They'd scoured the area around the cave for hours after venturing over to the smoldering remains of the jet. When they arrived, there wasn't much left other than scorched trees, earth, and about a four-foot section of the tail. They looked around for any signs of bodies yet found none. It was just sheer luck the machine slammed into an outcropping of shale, or the entire area would be engulfed in flames.

"Jesus, this is worse than we thought." Porterfield whispers. "The smoke is heavier toward Little Rock and Conway. Wonder if it's from them or us?"

"Does it really matter? I mean, destruction is destruction, no matter if the living or dead caused it."

Porterfield hands the binoculars back and Kevin returns them to his pack. "How far do you think we'll need to travel before we find us one for the doc? I didn't see any movement."

"Probably because they're too busy eating."

"There's a pleasant image. Not. And here I thought I was the one with the sick, twisted mind."

"Just stating obvious facts, dude."

Crouching down on a nearby rock, Kevin extracts two bottles of water and passes one to Porterfield. They each take a few sips while staring at the western sky. The sunset is magnificent and full of an array of colors.

He wishes it is a sign of better times to come yet knows the desire is a waste of headspace. "It's a shame we couldn't find a useful body in the wreckage. Guess that would've been too easy. Then again, none of them may have been sick."

"Oh, come on, Kevin! Of course one of them was sick. Why else would they have crashed?"

"Pilot error. Equipment malfunction. Medical emergency. Pick one."

Porterfield snorts. "Whatever. My gut tells me otherwise."

"Your gut isn't always right. Remember that time in Afghanistan?"

"Stop using that debacle as a weapon against me. I simply miscalculated. No harm, no foul."

"Uh-huh. I didn't buy it, and neither did our commander. Doubt those civvies who died would, either."

"Lay off, will you? We've got more important things to think about than something that happened years ago."

"You're right. Sorry. Let's just enjoy this sunset. Might be the last one we see for a while."

The conversation ends and for the next ten minutes, they watch the orange orb sink into oblivion in blessed silence. After the last rays of pink, blue, and yellow disappear, a heavy sense of dread fills Kevin's mind.

"You came down pretty hard on Dr. Berning earlier." He downs the final swig of water before turning his intense gaze on Porterfield. "When are you going to learn a show of might doesn't go as far as a softer touch?"

"Jesus, Warton. How well do you know me? I'm the same person I've always been, just edgier since all this happened. Time for changing these old spots is over."

"As long as you're breathing, change is always possible."

"Wow—when did you start reading liberal pamphlets? Make a trip to Berkley I didn't know about?"

"I'm just suggesting you go a bit easier on the old man. He did, after all, discover a cure for drug addiction, which no one else ever did. If anyone can solve what's going on, I'm putting all my money on his number."

"I'll continue to let you be the soft one." Porterfield laughs. "Somebody's got to play the heavy. Enough of this topic. Have you tried the radio again?"

Kevin shakes his head. "Not since we came topside."

"Try one more time."

Reaching his hand down into the pack he feels around for the radio, latches onto it, pulls it out and turns it to channel sixteen. "Mayday, mayday, anyone copy?"

Nothing.

Kevin's heart sinks.

Again.

"Guess we really are on our own." Porterfield closes his eyes for a split second while rubbing his temples. "Can't believe the world is ending and we don't even know why."

"Uh, we're still here, which means others are, too. If someone is still breathing, the fat lady hasn't sung her last tune."

"Hippy-talk. Say, now that we're alone, tell me why you lied earlier."

There isn't much light from the rising moon, yet Kevin sees the distrust behind Porterfield's eyes. "Come again?"

"Your brother-in-law. The Secret Service guy in D.C." Porterfield uses air quotes. "You don't have a sister, which is a requirement to have a brother-in-law. Who were you really talking to?"

Heat fills his cheeks as he kicks himself mentally for not covering his tracks better. For years, he'd kept the secret hidden from everyone, including his parents, who died without ever knowing the truth. Given the current situation, it seems trivial and pointless.

"It wasn't a lie. I was talking to my brother-in-law. He was married to my brother, Kent."

Porterfield's jaw drops. "You have a gay brother?"

"Had. Kent died five years ago. He was an agent, too, and feared losing his job if the brass found out he was gay. Jerry and I remained friends after Kent passed away. I was the only connection to Kent's family he had."

"Nice of you to support him. Not many would. Don't know if I could. Wait, not true. I wouldn't be able to get past...uh...certain things."

"To each their own. Thanks for not calling me out about it in front of the others. Guess it really doesn't matter anymore but old habits die hard."

"No worries. I've always got your back."

Unwilling to discuss the subject any longer, Kevin stands. "Let's get moving. Probably should head south, toward the closest town. Trekking through these woods in the dark is going to take a while."

"Wait." Porterfield rummages through his own pack. "Let's look at what's inside this little box before we go. Might have some intel we could use."

"Why didn't you tell me you found something at the crash site? We should've looked through this while the sun was still out!"

"Excuse me for not thinking straight. Consider it an apocalypse brain fart."

Kevin laughs. Porterfield has a wicked sense of humor. He yanks the flashlight from the clip on his belt and shines it down into the box. "That's all? Two cigars, a crumpled piece of paper and some blow?"

"You know those flyboys—they like to party. End-of-mission rewards and probably a love note from one of their many honeys. The cigar I get—the coke I don't. When did they stop testing pilots for drugs in the military?"

"Beats me." He shrugs while extracting a cigar. Rolling it in his fingers, he brings it to his nose and inhales. "Oh, this is a good one. Cuban, I think. Shall we, you know, before we head out?"

"Why not? Like the sunset, might be the last ones we come across in a long time."

Kevin searches his pack for matches. Just as his fingers latch around the small box, he hears Porterfield snort. He glances over and scowls. "No. You. Didn't. Why?"

Rubbing his nose, Porterfield takes another hit. "Why not? Waste not, want not, right? Besides, being wired will help keep me on my toes. Care to join me? It's no fun being high alone."

"No way. Never liked the stuff, and if Dirk finds out—oh, he's gonna beat your ass. May I remind you we worked for a doctor whose family died because of that shit, and started a project to end addiction?"

"Wow, come on down from that lofty mountain of superiority you're sitting on, Warton!" Porterfield chuckles. "Recall, we are living in a world full of dead people wandering around, which means life can be over any second. You're smoking a cancer stick, so what's the difference?"

"Nicotine won't cloud my judgment or ability to think when confronted by one of those walking corpses. That's the difference."

"Pussy."

"I lost my brother to that poison, asshole." His anger flares. "Kent used it as a crutch to deal with hiding his lifestyle from the world, and it killed him. That's why I came onboard when Dirk approached me. You're the pussy. Only the weak need something to help them cope with stress."

Porterfield ignores the comment and taps out another line.

"Take it easy, fool. Don't want you to fry those few remaining brain cells in your head. I'll need help carrying back our guest once we locate one."

Annoyed by his stupidity, Kevin refuses to watch him get high so he decides to read the note crammed inside the box.

Careful not to tear the thin paper, he smooths out the crinkled edges on his lap. The handwritten note is hard to read since the words look like they were penned by a ten-year-old:

When the high from the sky ends, this will keep you going! Merry Christmas from your friend across the border!

"Nice. What a way to keep diplomatic relations open." Kevin scowls.

Porterfield jumps to his feet while yanking his pack up onto his shoulder. "Time to move out. Let's go find us a nice, gooey one for Dr. Berning. I'll lay down a hundred bucks he passes out when he sees it!"

"That was quick. Stuff must be good." Kevin retorts, angry Porterfield made such a stupid choice. "Fine, but I'll lead the way. It'll force you to slow down. Oh, and you're on. Dr. Berning won't pass out—he'll puke. Guaranteed."

Both men laugh as they climb down the boulders and make their way through the forest. Kevin's skin crawls at the eerie silence. Lack of noise makes him wonder if animals are also susceptible to whatever disease lurks about.

"Damn, Kevin. This stuff is amazing. Haven't felt like this in years!"

"Stop talking and keep walking. We've got several miles to traverse until we reach the nearest town."

"I'm serious, dude! You should try some."

"Porterfield, your brain cells are diminishing quickly. I already told you why I won't. Remember?"

"You're missing out. The only thing that would make this experience better is a hot blonde with an insatiable libido to fuck until dawn. God, this takes me back to my college days."

Kevin ignores him and keeps walking, rifle slung over his shoulder. To his right, he hears leaves crackle as something big moves through the woods. His hand instinctively falls to the handgun holstered on his hip. He pulls it out and motions for Porterfield to stop.

"What's wrong?"

"Shhh. Didn't you hear that?"

Porterfield cocks his head in confusion. "That buzzing sound? You heard it to? Thank God, thought it was just me."

"No." The leaves continue crackling. "That."

"I...don't...hear...oh, man. My chest."

Porterfield collapses to his knees, clutching his chest. The noise from the woods picks up speed, heading west away from the duo. Kevin feels a sense of relief upon hearing a loud snort, recognizing the sound deer make when signaling danger to others.

"I told you not to hit it so hard. How long's it been since you tortured your system with blow?"

"Too…long…God, my heart is racing."

Kevin returns the gun to the holster and removes his pack. He grabs a bottle of water and a protein bar. "Here, drink some and take a few bites. When was the last time you ate?"

"Breakfast."

Rolling his eyes, he shoves the protein bar into Porterfield's shaking hand. "Idiot! Eat. Right now."

Porterfield takes a bite, chews, swallows, and then promptly falls onto all fours and throws it back up.

Kevin backs away from the torrent of vomit. "Thomas, I told you to be careful. Come on, you need to walk this off."

"Fuck you." Porterfield hisses.

Watching someone else puke always made Kevin fight the temptation to join them, so he turns his head. Though angry at Porterfield for bringing this onto himself, he also finds it sort of funny. "Okay, finish upchucking that shit out of your system and then let's head back to the cave. We can come back tomorrow and search again."

"You…smell…so…good."

The words are almost unintelligible. Kevin's chest tightens as his internal alarm bell warns something is wrong. His skin breaks out into a cold sweat and on instinct, he backs away from Porterfield several steps. After taking the fourth step, the hairs on his back, neck, and arms pop up when Porterfield raises his head and growls.

The thick clouds above part, and the moonlight reveals a white, frothy foam running down Porterfield's chin. His body jerks and writhes, making more spew from his mouth and nose. The white turns to dark pink in seconds as blood mixes with it.

"Stay right there. I mean it." Kevin orders. To enforce the words, he pulls out his gun and points it at his friend's head. "Talk to me. Tell me your name."

Porterfield collapses onto his stomach and quits moving.

"Good shit, huh?" He steps forward, intent on checking for a pulse, though he knows there won't be one because even from several feet away and in the dark, Porterfield is gone. "How in the world will I explain you overdosed on cocaine to Dirk?"

Porterfield springs to his feet.

Kevin stops in his tracks, stunned. "What the hell?"

His friend of fifteen years opens his mouth, growls again, and then lunges.

Kevin's training takes over. He fires one shot and the bullet rips through Porterfield's skull, knocking him backward. He crumples into a heap less than a foot away from Kevin's boots.

Shaking, breath coming in rasps, he stares at the gaping hole in the back of Porterfield's skull, gun still trained on the unmoving corpse. Taking several steps backward, he pulls out his flashlight.

The bright light, and what it illuminates, causes him to turn his head and puke. The retching isn't from the fact he just murdered his friend.

It is because Porterfield looks like all the others he's seen on television.

He was one of those things? How? Shit! Porterfield was contaminated, so does that mean he is, too? God, are they all just ticking time bombs?

He sinks to his knees, overwhelmed by the last twenty-four hours. The clouds reappear, blocking out the light of the moon. In the darkness, Kevin weeps until no tears remain.

After several minutes, he pulls himself together. Removing his jacket, he crawls next to what once had been his friend and wraps the material around his destroyed head.

"Guess you'll be making a contribution to science after all." He mutters while hefting Porterfield over his shoulder. "If I'm contaminated, too, looks like we both will."

Sanity long gone; he trudges through the dark forest back toward the cave. Porterfield's head thumps against his back with each step.

"Just like in Afghanistan when I saved your ass. The only difference is this time, you're dead. At the rate we're going, all of us will be joining you. Soon."

He hums "I've Been Working on the Railroad" which is the same song he sang while carrying the wounded Porterfield to safety through the desert. He cannot bring himself to sing out loud, since Porterfield isn't available to provide backup.

Chapter 16 - A New Home

Saturday, December 20th – 7:15 p.m.

MARTHA LOOKS OVER her shoulder and notices Turner stopped stroking Jesse's hair. The poor girl is finally asleep, stretched out in the back of the Humvee on top of mounds of supplies. For hours, she just stared at her feet, not uttering a sound, even when things got dicey a few times. Breathing a sigh of relief, she turns her attention to the window, thankful Jesse is getting some rest.

"She out?" Kyle asks in a low whisper.

"Yes." Turner answers from the back seat.

"Good. Let's pull over here and stretch our legs."

"And pee." Martha adds.

Kyle guides the Humvee over to the shoulder of Highway 9. Looking around, she notices the small, two-lane road is still empty. They haven't seen another vehicle, or any signs of life for that matter, since switching off Highway 65 in Clinton.

The emptiness is a blessing. They'd run into several issues on the way after fleeing Malvern. Though the original group of fifteen vehicles tried to steer clear of the clogged freeways and main thoroughfares, when they reached Conway via 286, they almost didn't make it any farther. Thousands of the dead and dying flooded the roadway like moving flood waters. She shudders, remembering how four vehicles were swarmed in seconds. Their screams of pain and terror still ring inside her mind and probably will haunt her dreams.

The other vehicles pull up in a single line behind them and everyone jumps out, yanking her back to grim reality. She touches Turner's arm. "You go first, honey. I'll watch Jesse until you get back."

The skin under Turner's eyes is dark and swollen. Worry lines cut a deep swath through his forehead, making him look much older than his actual age. She is glad there are no mirrors because she probably looks even worse.

"No, Mom. I've almost lost her twice today. Not leaving her side again. Ever."

"That's mighty admirable of you, son, but you need to take care of yourself, too. What good will you be to her if you fall apart?"

Turner squints his eyelids in irritation. "I doubt I'll fall ill from holding my bladder, Mom."

"Actually, I've heard waiting too long to piss causes problems later in life." Kyle teases. "Come on, Turner. Stretch. Eat. Fart outside, because God knows my nose hairs can't take another one of those paint-peelers inside the vehicle."

"You're hysterical, Kyle. Not." Turner claps back. "Stop trying to use humor to make things better. It isn't working."

"Enough. Get out and do your business. Eat. Just not anything gas-producing."

"Fine." Turner opens the door.

Martha waits until Kyle and Turner exit the vehicle before climbing over the seats to grab some water and toilet paper. Careful not to make any more noise than necessary so as not to wake Jesse, she gathers what she needs.

Once back in the front seat, she listens to the sounds of the others whispering outside. Her heart aches for Jesse and Reed. How they hadn't gone stark-raving mad after witnessing Regina blow her head off was by the grace of God.

Disgust rumbles in her stomach at the thought. She was glad she'd been out back with Turner and Kyle and missed the spectacle. Just thinking about the horrid scene brings back disturbing memories of her own childhood. Thirty-four years had passed since the day her life changed in her parents' living room, yet when something sparks the memory, it seems like only yesterday.

She remembers every sound, what everyone wore, even the television show blaring in the background when her father, drunk and in a foul mood as usual, started yelling, angry dinner was late. He rose from the recliner and stumbled into the kitchen. Martha stopped working on an English assignment and covered her ears when glass shattered and the sound of flesh smashing into flesh reached the living room.

What she didn't know—until it was too late to do anything about it—was it had been her mother who punched her father. The argument stopped and

Martha figured her mother was out cold on the kitchen floor—again—and her father had retreated to the garage.

He did, but he returned with a shotgun.

"No, don't go there, girl. Not today. I lack the strength to deal with the past because the present is a nightmare, too."

Forcing her thoughts elsewhere—rather than reliving the night her father killed her mother—she stares out the window, watching those she's loved for years intermingle between the ones she's come to cherish.

She holds in tears at the memory of Walt, Reed, and Kyle bursting out the back door of Walmart, a hysterical Jesse firmly secured in Reed's arms...

...Residents flooded the back parking area, arms full of supplies.

When the shooting started seconds before, Martha, Turner, and Kyle shut the doors on the Humvees they were loading and tried to head back inside to help, but the throng of panicked people were like ants on a forgotten piece of candy, swarming out the doors going in circles until they found their vehicles and took off.

Walter and Jane stopped to aide an injured child and got separated from the group. Turner punched out a young kid blocking his way to Jesse. Reed burst through the crowd, Turner right at his side, and Kyle yanked Martha backward into the Humvee.

"We've got to leave, right now! Look!" Kyle yelled while locking the doors.

"I'm not leaving without my husband!" Martha screamed, clawing at the lock.

"Look, Dad's fine." Turner pointed out the window. "He made it to a vehicle."

Martha rolled down the window and heard Walt's booming voice. "Hospital! Now!"

Kyle guided the Humvee through the nightmare that was once Walmart's parking lot. Cars full of panicked drivers ran into each other while trying to jockey for a better position or dodge the dead. Those in small sedans—so popular with the younger generation—didn't stand a chance against hungry monsters. The large section of blacktop was like a bigger version of the bumper car ride at the county fair. The second a car collided with another; the dead swooped in like two-legged vultures.

Martha tried to help. She rolled the window down and fired at the dead. Riding in a vehicle as it zigzagged through the parking lot made her miss more than she connected. By the time they passed the smoldering remains of the Humvees, hundreds of dead crouched down and eating the remains of the soldiers, she was out of bullets, unable to end the suffering of those still alive.

Jesse's screams of agony for the loss of her mother morphed into deep, racking sobs by the time they arrived at the hospital. When they stopped, Martha jumped out, noting fifteen vehicles pulled in behind them, all escapees from the store. Ignoring them, she ran to Walt's Humvee, throwing her arms around his neck after he stepped out.

"Thought you were a goner," she whispered into his chest. "Don't ever scare me like that again."

"Lover—it's gonna take more than some dead corpse to take me out." Walt kissed her forehead.

"God, it's all gone! Look at that." Jane muttered.

Turning around, they watched in silent horror as plumes of thick smoke rose from the vicinity of Walmart's parking lot. The bursts of gunfire stopped, and the only noise left was the faint, distant screams of those who hadn't escaped.

They thought the destruction and massive loss of life at Walmart was awful, but it paled in comparison to the carnage they discovered inside the hospital.

The small, 72-bed facility was nothing more than a tomb for hundreds of murder victims. Spent shell casings littered the floors, firmly stuck in several inches of tacky, dark blood.

Jane and Kyle volunteered to extract all the medical supplies they could carry while the rest of the group headed back outside. When Walt broke the news no one was alive inside, wails of sorrow rumbled through the crowd. Pastor Trent stepped forward, tears running down his face while making his way to the entrance before offering prayers.

No one joined him.

They were too overwhelmed to move.

Time to mourn the dead ended when Jane and Kyle exited the building. A swarm of dead appeared from the side streets. Walt screamed, "If you want to a safe place to stay follow me!"…

…Martha sighs, knowing she'll never see the place she called home her entire life again. The good, the bad, and the oh-so ugly memories are all that is left.

Jesse stirs, bringing Martha out of her ruminations. She turns around in the seat to see if the girl is awake or just shifting positions.

"Momma." Jesse whimpers.

The side door opens, and Turner slips back inside. "Shhh, baby. It's okay. I'm here. Go back to sleep."

Jesse falls silent once again the second Turner's hand touches her back.

Exchanging glances with her son, Turner nods and mouths, *"Your turn."*

Martha slips out the door, toilet paper in hand. The view of the mountain range used to bring a sense of serenity and peace every time she saw it. In the dark, surrounded by hungry, heartbroken, dirty stragglers, the serene feelings are long gone.

Spotting Reed up ahead, she moves forward. He stands, his back to her, staring in the direction they'd come. He hasn't spoken much during the last several hours, and the opportunity to offer her condolences hasn't surfaced while they fled their hometown.

Clearing her throat to announce her presence, she comes up behind him and stops, figuring Reed is crying and decides to give him the chance to pull himself together. "I'm so sorry about what happened to Regina. She was a great woman. A true hero."

Her instincts were right. Reed reaches up and wipes his face several times on his sleeve before turning around. Even in the dark, she sees the look of anguish on his face. "Yes, she was. Thank you."

"She had the right idea, you know. We could've holed up there for quite some time. Others just screwed it up."

"Yeah, some people are just pieces of shit."

"Yes, they are, but we can't let that taint our views on everyone."

"I'm not so sure about that, Martha. Not sure at all."

"I am. Lived through some dark times in my life, as I'm sure you recall. Thought things would never get better, but then I met my Walter. Silver linings in the storm clouds sometimes appear out of nowhere. Or, in my case, transfer schools."

"I remember." Reed smiles. "You two hit it right off. Didn't you guys get voted best couple or some such nonsense?"

"Yep. And Regina was voted most likely to succeed. She lived up to that and more."

"Too bad no one will know what she sacrificed..." He stops in mid-sentence when his voice cracks.

"We know. And that's enough."

He takes a deep breath and nods while glancing to the left. "Excuse me, Martha. Need to talk to Kyle for a few minutes before we finish our journey. Thank you for the kind words."

She watches Reed walk away and over to Kyle before stepping behind a tree, doing her business, and then rejoins the others. They are all huddled at the back of Walt's vehicle. She detects tension in the voices speaking as she approaches.

"Are you serious? Now? Up here? Not a good idea, pastor. Not a good idea".

"Mr. Addison, my wife, and some of the others, have family in West Plains, Missouri. It's less than one-hundred miles from here. We'll just continue on this highway until we make it."

"What if you run into more trouble?" Kyle asks.

Pastor Trent smiles. "We haven't seen a soul on this road in hours, so I doubt that will change anytime soon. The population is slim up here. Besides, the Lord will watch over us."

"Yeah, he's done a great job of that so far." Reed counters.

"Actually, He has. You all saved our lives back at the school, which gave us a chance to make it this close to our remaining family with a vehicle full of supplies and armed escorts. What more could He have done?"

"A lot!" Reed explodes. "For starters, not letting people turn into fucking monsters! Oh, and let's not forget how quickly the living turned into selfish bastards who fled at the first signs of danger. I'm not sure what's worse—the dead eating the living, or the living slaughtering the living!"

"Son, the only thing that's changed in this world from the deplorable state it was in before is the dead rose and walk again. Humanity's inhumanity toward others is still the same, no matter the cause."

Closing the space between them, Reed's inches from the elderly pastor. "That's the biggest load of shit I've ever heard!"

Walt steps forward to intervene, but Martha beats him to it. She put both hands on Reed's heaving chest. "Reed—go check on Jesse. Now."

"Crazy fools." Reed mutters while walking away.

Turning back to Pastor Trent, Martha softens her tone. "I understand your decision, and we'll pray for y'all to make it safely. Do you have enough gas?"

"And ammo?" Walt adds.

Pastor Trent nods. "Yes, thank you. Another blessing from above was not only these big, safe vehicles, but ones full of extra gas. Again, thank you. For everything. Safe travels, my friends. God bless."

She grabs Walt's hand and squeezes, stopping him from saying anything else. In seconds, seven vehicles pull back onto the highway led by the pastor and head north on Highway 9.

"Ain't no way they'll survive." Kyle shakes his head. "I agree with Reed. Crazy fools."

"Don't judge others for their decisions until you know their reasons."

"Martha, I know their reasons. They wanted our help—took it—and then left when things got tough."

"You're wrong, Walt. Jolene has ovarian cancer. Stage Four. They just found out last week. Planned on announcing it at church on Sunday during prayer request time."

"How do you know, then?" Walt looks dubious.

"Jolene told me back at Walmart. She's got a month—tops. Can you blame her for wanting to be surrounded by family when she goes?"

"No, I guess not." Walt sighs.

"Okay, so our group shrunk a bit." Kyle rubs his jaw. "Means we can drive faster. How much farther to the cave, Walt?"

"About forty miles. If we don't run into any trouble, we should arrive by nine. Then another hour or so on foot."

"Foot? At night?" Kyle rolls his eyes. "Oh, this will be fun."

"And dangerous." Martha adds. "Stick together and stay alert. We're all in this together now."

***

Sure enough, her husband was right on target. They arrive and park in empty spots at the deer camp at ten after nine.

Not a word was spoken after they left the pit stop on the side of the road, even when Martha passed out water and food. Each were lost inside their shattered minds, wondering what awaited them in the dark, and busy searching the roads for any signs of life.

Or the dead.

Kyle shuts the engine down. Martha looks back at Jesse, who's been awake for the last half-hour. The girl looks like hell, and she's concerned about her state of mind, so she keeps her tone light. "Come on, let's gather what we can carry and head out."

People stream out of the remaining four vehicles, all busying themselves with grabbing supplies. The ragtag group of Martha, Walt, Turner, Jesse, Reed,

Kyle, Lamar, and the others work quickly, securing items while simultaneously keeping watch on the woods.

Walt moves next to her and swipes a kiss on her cheek before grabbing the pack of food and water from her hands. "Let me take those. I need your expert marksmanship skills to keep us safe. I'll lead."

Nodding in agreement, she grabs a box of shells and reloads her rifle. "Turner? Make sure to pack the remaining bullets in your bag."

"On it.".

Door's lock and feet shuffle as the group of fifteen gathers in a semi-circle. Shaun Kilpatrick steps forward, rifle dangling from his chest. His clothes are covered in dark, dried blood, and the haunted, sad look on his face makes her cringe.

"How far?" Shaun nods toward the forest.

"About five klicks north." Walt takes a deep breath. "The trail's thin and treacherous. Watch your footing. Form a single line behind me and don't veer from the trail. Cliffs are steep up here, and just one misstep will send you bouncing down the hillside."

"You're sure there's room for us all?" Bailey asks.

"Wouldn't have brought y'all up here if I had any doubts." Walt glances once at her and she detects the tension in his jaw. "Come on, enough chit-chat. We're exposed out here and need to get moving."

Rather than wait for any responses, he turns from the crowd and heads toward the trail. As instructed, the others follow, forming a single line.

Her gaze bounces from one side to the other, glad her vision adapted to the darkness so quickly. Though she is way past forty, she still has the eyes of a teenager.

The night air is cold. The temperature in the mountains is lower than in the valley. By the time they trek a mile, her eyes are watering. Judging by the numbness in her cheeks, she guesses it is below freezing.

They are on a stretch of the trail with an incline, and everyone is breathing hard. No one speaks, using all their strength to keep moving forward. She doesn't want to dwell on the horrors from earlier, so she silently counts each step.

They are close to the two-mile mark when Walt grinds to a halt. "Hold up."

"What's wrong?"

"We ain't alone, Martha." He squats down and peers at the ground in front of him. She follows his gaze as Kyle steps past her, flashlight in hand.

"What's that?" she asks.

"Dried blood and brain matter. Look there, Martha. What do you see?" Walt points left.

"Bullet casing. Shit."

"Yep." Kyle sighs. "Someone's got their brains blown out."

"Maybe a hunter bagged a deer?"

"No, honey." Walt shakes his head. "Deer ain't got that much brain matter."

"Oh, shit! You think maybe someone killed an infected?" Kyle asks.

"No. Where's the corpse?" Walt stands and takes a few steps forward, retrieving a backpack. "I certainly wouldn't stop and bury a monster I'd just shot. I'd be too busy running. This corpse took a ride on the back of whomever shot it. See the indentations there, and there? Only one set of prints, and either they were made by someone very overweight, or someone carrying another."

"Thought you said this place of yours was safe and no one knew about it?" Shaun grouses.

"I did, and it is." Walt rummages through the pack. "Dammit, I knew I was right!"

Turner peers closer. "Military issue?"

Martha looks behind her and notices everyone has crammed together. She feels their collective anxiety as though a living entity.

"Yep. Son, I told you those tracks we saw two years ago were from some government fool."

Martha senses her husband is close to full meltdown. "Well, they ain't here now and can't get into our cave, so let's stop gabbing and get moving before someone, or *something*, hears us."

Walt tosses the pack aside, nodding in agreement. "Bastards better steer clear of this side of the mountain."

Picking up their pace, the group make it to the entrance of the cave in twenty minutes. Walt and Turner clear the brush and limbs from the opening and unlock the padlock securing the heavy metal door Martha helped him install years ago.

"Hang on while I get the generator going." Walt

disappears inside the dark cavern and seconds later, the generator purrs to life. A faint glow of yellow shines from the doorway.

"Come on, hurry," she urges.

The others speed past her, unwilling to remain out in the cold, dark woods any longer. Deputy Bailey is the last one inside. She shuts the door and secures the metal bar across it before joining the others.

"Wow, some spread you got here, Walt." Kyle lets out a low whistle. "Cots, bedding, jars of food, light. Better than some hotels I've stayed at."

"Let me give you a quick tour. We've got about six thousand square feet down here. Behind that wall over there is a latrine. Blankets, bedding, and pillows are inside those six containers. Only ten cots, so some of you will be in sleeping bags on the floor. Water goes there, and food over there." Walt points toward the dark recesses behind him. "Let's get set up and some shut eye. We all need rest."

The group works in tandem, and in minutes, the mattresses are covered in sheets and blankets, sleeping bags resting next to them, and the food and water stowed. Bladders are emptied. Though the cave is cold, it is warmer than outside, and the energy exuded from fifteen moving bodies helped raise the temperature.

The husband-wife prepper duo finish stacking up the remaining supplies when Reed approaches.

"Thank you. For everything. Jesse and I owe you a debt we can never repay."

"No need to thank us." Martha smiles. "This is what friends do—help one another."

"But we ain't always been friends, more like distant acquaintances."

"Well, we are now. Considering how much those two are in love, we're practically family." Walt nods to the right.

Martha looks over at the young love birds. Turner makes sure Jesse is warm and snug on a cot before crawling into a sleeping bag right by her side. The love between them fills the room and her heart swells with pride.

Fifteen minutes later, the generator turned off to save gas, and no sounds but the steady breathing of fourteen exhausted others drifting off to sleep, Martha clasps Walt's hand. "I love you, Walter Addison. Thank you for being ready."

"For you, the world. Goodnight, my love."

Chapter 17 - Unearthing the Cause

Sunday, December 21st – 3:15 a.m.

EVERETT STARES IN SHOCK through the small lens of the microscope. It is the second time in his life he's been stunned into awed silence inside the lab. The first time had been a joyous moment when discovering something capable of changing the course of human history. The current one is so horrendous, he lacks words to describe it, though it has the same capability in terms of how it will affect those still alive.

Leaning back, he grabs the photocopies he found while rummaging around in Dr. Flint's office earlier. While waiting for Warton and Porterfield to return, he couldn't stand reading any longer, so he busied himself by rifling through her office. When he found a hidden slat underneath her desk and extracted a folder filled with piles of paper, he wanted to kick himself for not searching sooner.

Inside the folder is a goldmine. It contains a clean, clear copy of the last three months of his handwritten notes before the discovery, including the chemical formula of batch 10,899.

Hand shaking, he flips to the page with the formula and then sets it back down and picks up the printout with the results from running a sample through the GC-MS machine. Comparing the two pieces of paper, his stomach drops. He almost wishes Daryl would have destroyed the Gas Chromatography-Mass Spectrometry machine like he did to the computers because the results make his head spin.

"Son-of-a-bitch!"

Refusing to look any more, he rises and leaves the lab. He needs to hear all the details from Warton on what exactly Porterfield was doing before he turned. He must make sure he is right before explaining his findings to the remaining five soldiers.

He takes a few steps down the hall before changing directions and running to the bathroom and pukes, overwhelmed by the heavy weight of the discovery. After retching and washing his face, he nearly laughs. He'd kept it together when Warton brought in Porterfield's dead body, holding back the vomit while helping to extract blood samples. He'd been proud of himself for not showing any signs of weakness in front of the others, but his pride disappeared the second he viewed the results. Now, he is overcome with shame, guilt, and remorse crushing down on his heart and soul, crushing him underneath the weight.

Stepping back out into the hallway, he trudges forward until reaching the common area where Dirk and the others took up residence. Pausing at the door, he lets out a long sigh.

How in the world can I tell them the truth? Maybe I'll get lucky and they'll all be asleep. I could just run away. Snag a set of keys and sneak topside. Better yet! Find one of their guns and blow my head off first before one of them gets the chance to beat me to it.

Opening the door, he steps inside, heart racing. He spots Dirk first, who is quietly talking to Kevin Warton on the far side of the room. Warton is still dressed in the filthy clothes he had on before, his face devoid of emotion.

Crossing the room, he sits across from the two men. The remaining soldiers follow and sit around the table. He wonders if they sense his fear. "Tell me every detail of what happened to Mr. Porterfield."

Warton raises his head, a set of bloodshot eyes stare back, full of pain and anger. "What's there to tell? We went up, Thomas got sick, tried to attack me, and I shot him. End of story."

"Did he exhibit any signs of being ill before he turned or say anything at all about how he felt or give any indication something was wrong? Was he sweating or in pain?"

"Why does it matter now? You wanted a sample; I brought you one. Plain and simple."

"Warton, breathe." Dirk urges. "I know it's hard, but even the smallest detail might help the Doc."

Kevin rises, pacing back and forth in front of the table. Everett grimaces at the dried tissue and blood embedded in the back of his jacket.

"Details? You want the gory details? Fine. We went up, scoured the wreckage, and found nothing except a small, metal box. Porterfield opened it, we each snatched a cigar, and he snorted some blow from inside. A present from some low-life flyboy fan from across the border. I tried to stop him, but he wouldn't listen. He took three hits of the stuff and then we started down the mountainside. Within ten minutes, he was puking his guts out. He fell over after his heart gave out and then he popped back up and tried to eat me. There. How's that for fucking details? Care to know if I threw up, too? Or cried like a baby after shooting my friend right between his black, fucked up eyes?"

Everett's stomach roils again so he closes his eyes and fights the urge to vomit. What he wants—needs—to hear, is missing from Warton's description. He's been praying in silence the entire time, hoping Kevin wouldn't mention drugs. Hearing the words crushed what little sanity remained inside his mind.

"Doc? What's wrong? What did you discover in there?" Dirk asks.

Afraid of what the reaction will be from the others when he answers, he forces himself to stand. He doesn't want his life to end while sitting in a plastic chair. "Several things, Dirk, and none of them are good."

"We didn't expect them to be, so please continue."

"I don't know if I can. It's just...too surreal."

"Porterfield's dead because you needed a fucking sample!" Kevin yells. "And since I'm the one who ended his life, I think I earned the right to hear why he turned!"

To bring his point home, Kevin smashes his fist on the table. All the metal cups and utensils used earlier rattle. Everett bites his lip to keep from jumping in fright.

"You're right, Kevin. So, here's what I know." He takes a deep breath. "The sample of blood and tissue revealed traces of transgenic bacteria and the Rhabdovirus encased inside fungus. There were also high amounts of benzoylmethlecgonine."

"Fucking English, Doc!" Kevin explodes. "What does any of that mean?"

Dirk cocks an eyebrow. "Rhabdovirus? Doc, is that any way related to rabies? That certainly would explain a lot."

"Yes. And benzoylmethlecgonine is the clinical term for cocaine. I needed to know how much time transpired between Thomas ingesting some and turning."

"Are you trying to tell us the cocaine turned Porterfield into a zombie?" Kevin's mouth gapes open. "That's even more ridiculous than saying the word zombie! What the fuck's wrong with you, Doc?"

"What's wrong with me? What's wrong with me?" Everett yells as the weight of the situation bursts out of him. "I'll tell you what's wrong. The reason Porterfield's skin looks like the root system of a tree took up residence underneath it is because that's exactly what it is: a root system. A fungal network coursed through his body and took control of everything, and just like in a plant system, chemical signals pass through the networks. That's what reanimated Porterfield—and all the others. A fucking fungal infection took over and simply used the body as a means of transport in search of food."

"You're insane!" Kevin collapses onto the chair next to him. "Certifiable. That's impossible."

"Three days ago, I would've agreed one hundred percent, but after opening him up and seeing those fungal filaments functioning as vascular and neural networks, I changed my mind."

"Okay, let's all calm down here." Dirk's voice is calm yet stern. "Doc, if you believe some sort of funky, fungal infection is the cause of the problem, did you determine if it's contagious? Is it airborne? How is it transmitted? Are we all at risk?"

Though he wants to answer Dirk's questions with a lie, the scientist inside him won't allow it. "At first, I thought so, but after discovering cocaine was in Porterfield's system, and verifying the facts he ingested some from Kevin's recollections, we're fine. Transmission occurs from ingestion of a substance with the infection, or through exchange of bodily fluids."

"Gee, that's good to know." Kevin snorts derisively. "As long as none of us get high or sustain a bite, we're fine. Awesome."

"Seems to me your concern level isn't too high, Mr. Wharton, because you're still wearing contaminated clothing."

"Fuck you, old man!"

Everett turns his attention to Dirk. "Recall the night you rescued me in Laredo and stopped me from grabbing the bag Daryl had with him?"

"Yes, but how does that come into play?"

"Riverside had five vials of the serum, along with a flash drive containing the chemical formula of the cure I discovered. Those same exact chemical markers are in Porterfield's blood."

"Jesus H. Christ! What are you saying, Doc?"

"Dirk, what I'm trying to say is whomever Riverside was working for got their hands on the formula. Maybe someone else did. I don't know. My educated guess would be whomever found it, tweaked, and added things, such as the virus, maybe hoping they could reverse the formula. Make it more potent. Since they used the rabies virus, I figure they wanted to create something to make drugs more addictive. How the fungus fits in I'm not quite sure and won't be until more research is conducted. Could be simple contamination from a dirty lab."

Kevin's face turns red. Bursting from the seat, he lunges for Everett, hands outstretched, spittle flying from his mouth. "It's all your fault, you stupid, stupid old man!"

He doesn't move or try to outmaneuver Kevin's onslaught, opting to remain still, close his eyes, and wait for the impact.

I deserve to die for what I've done. What I created. I ended the world.

Kevin's cold fingers find his throat and squeeze. They fell backward, toppling over the table. Chairs fall over and the remaining men yell, Dirk the loudest, to release him.

He never raises a hand to fight back, not even when stars dance in front of his eyes, embracing the end, grateful his wretched life is almost over.

The pressure ends and Everett sucks in a lungful of air.

"Walk it off, Warton. Now." Dirk commands.

The sounds of a scuffle of boots on the floor reverberate all around him as he tries to stand. The leg he'd taken a bullet in last year is bent at an odd angle and throbs with burning, white-hot pain.

A warm hand reaches down and grabs his arm. "Come on, Doc. Get up. He's gone."

Everett opens his eyes as Dirk assists him off the floor. He glances at each man, and the horrified looks on their faces, especially Dirk's, make him wish they would have just let Warton finish him off.

***

Teresa Alvarado wakes with a start to the sound of heavy footsteps above. Goosebumps appear on her arms.

"Roberto?"

No response.

Dashing to the window, she peers out, immediately clamping her fingers over her mouth to keep from screaming when seeing several men dressed in uniforms in the yard.

"Roberto? Where are you?" she whispers again.

She doesn't have time to search for her missing fiancé because the footsteps are right outside the door. Heart pounding and tears running down her face, she looks for a place to hide. The only thing she can fit in is the old trunk she had shipped from home full of all her favorite trinkets from her childhood bedroom.

Crouching next to it, she opens the lid. There is just enough room for her to slide inside. Her hands shake and refuse to obey her mind to close the top. Fighting off the claustrophobia, spurred on by the shouts of men from above, she overrides the fear and closes the lid.

Shoving her fist into her mouth, she bites down hard enough to draw blood, so she doesn't scream.

The door bursts open and what sounds like four separate sets of boots rush inside. She bites down harder. Silent tears roll, soaking her hair and dripping into her ears.

"Check everywhere. We can't leave anyone alive. This is the last house. Hopefully the bastard who escaped earlier was the final straggler."

"Yeah, well he didn't last long. Wasn't much left of him by the time you shot him, Garcia."

Tremors of sadness and fear grip her chest like a crushing vice. Roberto is dead—and he left her alone. How could he do such a thing to the woman he was to marry? Why didn't he wake her? The man swore his undying love, but it was all a lie. Pendejo bastard deserved death.

Her bladder gives way to fear when she realizes one of the soldiers is right next to the trunk. *Please, God. Don't let him open the lid! Please! I don't want to die. Not here. Not alone. I just want to find my sister and go home.*

"Clear down here. Let's head out."

The footsteps retreat up the stairs. Unable to control her muscles, the shakes set in. One of the men from the first-floor yells, "Got two infected up here. Looks like our escapee bagged them a while ago. Wonder why he stayed inside so long before leaving?"

Another man responds, but Teresa cannot make out the words. Straining her ears, she waits inside the dark prison until the last set of boots ceases making noise upstairs. She remains in the trunk for an extra five minutes in case they are hiding, waiting for her to appear, before she pushes the lid open.

Tiptoeing across the floor, she looks out the window. The soldiers are gone, along with the big trucks previously parked in the street. Collapsing to her knees, she buries her head into the thin mattress she'd been sleeping on to stifle her screams of anguish.

When the screams cease, she wraps her arms around her legs and curls into a ball in the corner, madness and terror controlling every thought.

What now? Roberto left and didn't make it, so how will I survive?

***

Hours later, sunlight no longer fills the basement with light. Teresa uncurls her stiff limbs and stands, driven by hunger and thirst to walk up the stairs. She shuffles into the kitchen after stumbling and falling several times in the dark, opens the fridge door, and gags at the stench of rotting food. She feels around until her fingers touch the familiar shape of a water bottle.

Twisting off the cap, she downs the entire twenty-four ounces. The tepid liquid helps her regain a sense of balance, so she makes her way to the den, where she knows her traitorous, chicken-shit fiancé keeps guns and ammunition.

Bare feet slapping against the cool tiles, she trips over the shattered front door and the once-beautiful decorations strewn across the floor. The military men destroyed her lovely house and oddly, she doesn't care. The only thing she cares about—what drives her to keep putting one foot in front of the other—is getting armed and in a vehicle.

She must find Maria. Teresa is the older sister, so it is her job to take care of her, and there doesn't seem to be anyone else available to help.

Less than ten feet away from the door leading to the den, she's accosted with the smell of rotting flesh. The stench brings her back to the time when she and Maria played at the edge of the jungle years ago and found the carcass of a dead animal.

Burying her nose in the crook of her arm, she keeps moving. The house is dark, but her eyes have adjusted enough she can pick out the white of the walls to use as a guide. Something hard connects with her toe. Wincing, she shifts directions, running straight into the couch. Blood on her hands from her earlier falls make her hands slip off the slick leather, and she falls.

When she realizes she has landed on top of a body, something inside her mind snaps.

I'm still alive. Stop freaking out. I'm going to run into more like them from now on. If I want to survive—to find Maria—I'll need to pretend this is just a dream. A dream in which I'm a badass afraid of nothing. Get up. Find the safe and get the guns.

Gritting her teeth, she pushes herself off the body and floor, only to freeze when it dawns on her what her toe had touched earlier. Squatting back down on all fours, she fumbles around until finding it.

"Yes!"

The gun is cold and heavy, yet feeling the weight in her hand gives her renewed strength.

She shuffles over to the wall, careful not to pick up her feet, and breathes a sigh of relief when she touches the metal safe, but the second she feels around inside, her heart rate spikes.

"You took the gun *and* the bullets, leaving me with nothing! I hate you, Roberto Sanchez. Damn you!"

In a panic, she continues feeling around, praying she is wrong, but she isn't. The only items left inside are a few wads of cash, a binder, and empty boxes of shells. Reaching her arm all the way inside, desperate to find another gun, she cries out when her fingers touch something else.

Pulling it free, the excitement of thinking it was a gun disappears. It is only a flashlight.

"Better than nothing."

She considers turning it on yet worries the light will be seen by any remaining soldiers in the area. She stuffs the cash and the binder into her waistband and leaves the den, hoping her purse is still in the kitchen.

To her relief, it is, so she grabs it and darts out the side door into the garage. Holding the gun in trembling fingers, she makes her way to the Navigator while watching for signs of anyone—dead or alive—lurking in the shadows.

Seeing nothing, and hearing only faint screaming in the distance, Teresa creeps through the garage, not realizing she's been holding her breath until she lets it out in a huge *whoosh* once reaching the door to the vehicle.

Once inside the SUV, she tosses the money and binder onto the passenger seat and starts the vehicle, wincing when the dashboard lights come on. Only a half-tank of gas remains.

"Won't get very far on that. Okay, think. Baby steps. Get out of the city. Stay on the main roads. Find a gas station and food. Then, figure out the best place to start looking for Maria."

Plan of action in place, she shifts the gear into reverse and backs out of the driveway, leaving the lights off, and maneuvers the Navigator through the mess left on her street, dodging bodies, and vehicles as she drives.

"Don't look at them. Ignore the blood. The dead. Don't try to help anyone. You don't have enough bullets. Just drive until you find Maria."

In the darkness, fear pulsing throughout her entire body, the words become her new mantra and she repeats them over and over to keep herself from screaming.

Chapter 18 - First Dawn in a New World

Sunday, December 21st – 4:25 a.m.

JESSE JERKES AWAKE from a horrid dream. The sound of the gunshot that ended her mother's life reverberates inside her mind even after opening her eyes. Covered in sweat and shaking, she sits up and tries to calm down.

Looking around the area makes her chest tighten. Though surrounded by others and plenty of room, the walls are closing in. The sensation of being trapped rises from deep within her belly, spreading quickly. Her breathing comes in short rasps. A panic attack is seconds away.

Careful not to make a sound, she rises from the cot, stepping away from the others. After clearing the sleeping bodies, her heartrate spikes.

I've got to get outta here. Need fresh air. Open space.

Forcing herself not to run, she makes it to the door and slips outside. A rush of cold air slaps her in the face, helping to cool the flames bubbling underneath her skin. The freezing air slices through the thin coat and pajamas faster than if she dove into ice water. After taking in several gulps of air and staring up into the dark, starless sky, the pending panic attack vanishes.

Turning back to the door, she hesitates, not quite ready to go back inside. Instead, she starts walking, hoping the crisp air will blast away the remaining traces of the nightmare.

She cannot grasp the fact her mom is gone. Not only is she dead, but she killed herself to save others. No burial. No mourning relatives or friends will ever come to pay their final respects to a woman who went above and beyond the call of duty for ungrateful strangers. There is no time for Jesse to grieve, or a place to visit and set fresh flowers in remembrance.

Nothing.

Her mother's body is probably all gone now, nothing left but bones and clothes strewn down aisle six of Walmart Supercenter in Malvern, Arkansas, and right next to the gnawed remains of Marian Kilpatrick and the baby girl she didn't want.

And the body of the stupid soldier.

Why did Shaun risk his life to save a man who had been part of the problem? The time Jane wasted on the bastard could have been spent on her mom. Then again, how could the soldiers have been so callous, so ready to blindly follow orders, and kill innocent people?

How in the hell had the world turned into a living nightmare in less than forty-eight hours?

She'd been a huge fan of movies, TV shows, and books about zombies, squealing with disgust when gory scenes happened, cheering when favorite characters did something heroic, or survived an impossible scenario to live on in the next episode. But that was all make-believe, Hollywood driven, green-screen magic. The actors covered in fake blood, brain matter, limbs broken and flesh missing, weren't real. She watched the unreal carnage and blood baths because it made her forget about the horrible things she'd endured when on the streets as a struggling junkie.

This nightmare is real, and she cannot handle reality, which is why she became a drug addict years ago.

Is this it? The real way the world ends, just not with some director yelling, "Cut!" when an actor blew their lines, or a piece of the set fell? How much longer can they last, holed up in a fucking *cave* for God's sakes, before the dead find them? Even if they are safe for the foreseeable future, what kind of life will it be? Scrounging around in the forest for food, making dangerous trips to formally populated locations to search for more supplies?

"No. No way. I'm not going to live like that. I'm not a rat!"

Jesse breaks out into a full run. After the few hundred yards, she loses her slippers, but she refuses to let the cold, or the pebbles and tree roots digging into her bare feet, impede her. She doesn't think about Turner or Uncle Reed or any of the others back at the cave.

First Dad, now Mom. I'm an orphan in a world that doesn't have much time left.

Images of Susie blowing her head off, whimpering for her mother before she pulled the trigger, bring more tears while thinking about the strange connection she feels to the girl. Susie lamented the loss of everything she'd even known, all her loved ones gone, and was left alone in a cruel, ugly world.

No pausing this episode. No ability to switch channels.

Stumbling down the dark path, no sounds except her own heavy breathing and whimpers, she pushes her muscles to their limit, ignoring the sting of tree limbs smacking her face and tearing at her clothes. Where she is going—or how long she'll run—doesn't enter her mind. She just pumps her arms and legs at full speed, tears clouding her vision.

Suddenly, she is in the air, body launched several feet after tripping over a dark mass on the trail. She lands hard on her left side, her back muscles from the earlier strain of carrying her mother, screaming. Her head smashes into a rock, and for the first time since she's ventured outside, sees stars.

It takes several minutes to regain control of her muscles. The ground is freezing. When she moves, she realizes she's lost her jacket somewhere, and her pajama top is bunched up around her waist, the bare skin of her back exposed.

When she tries to move, it feels like hundreds of bee stings burn into her back. Ignoring the pain, she forces herself to stand, looks around, and wonders how far she'd run. Nothing looks familiar, but then again, she didn't expect to see anything she'd recognize. Though she heard Turner mention the cave is near Blanchard Springs, she has never been up in this part of the state before.

Spent, body sore and cold, there is no choice except to head back to the cave. Her little temper-tantrum is over, and the run helped release some of the stress bottled up inside her head. She limps back the way she came, noticing the dark mass of what she'd tripped over earlier to the right.

She stops and stares at it, grateful for the first rays of the early morning sun streaking across the sky, recognizing it immediately. It is the backpack Walter found earlier while they trekked to the cave.

"Government. He said it had something to do with the government. Maybe there's a radio or supplies we can use inside."

Squatting down, she grabs the pack. The pine trees above her form a living canopy, blocking out the early morning light. She hobbles over to a boulder on the right, one coated in the warm rays of the sun.

"Please let there be something useful in here."

Digging through the canvas bag, she finds a lighter, a half-smoked cigar, a huge knife, a couple bottles of water, a map of Arkansas, extra rounds of ammunition, some protein bars, and a small metal box.

"What's in here?"

Fumbling to get the latch open, her determination is rewarded. Her eyes widen when seeing the treasure hiding inside.

"Please be meth. Please be meth!"

Snatching up the baggie, she licks a finger and sticks it inside. Just like in the jail, she doesn't really care what it is except that the white stuff is strong enough to give her a few hours of mind-numbing bliss.

"What the hell are you doing?"

The sound of a male voice makes her jump. The baggie slips from her fingers to the ground, white powder shooting in all directions. "Damnit! You just ruined...you scared the daylights of out me, Shaun. What are *you* doing out here?"

Shaun steps out of the shadows and over to the boulder. "I asked you first."

Standing, using her feet to displace the rest of the powder, she clears her throat. "I needed some fresh air. Claustrophobic."

"Yeah, me too. Plus, I saw you slip out and thought you might need protection. You know, with all that's going on?"

"Nice try. Chivalry ended generations ago. I can take care of myself, so you should head back."

"What's that?"

She holds up the pack. "You mean this?"

"Yep. Looks like the bag Walter found earlier on our way up here."

She steps away from the boulder and back onto the trail. "That's because it is. I was just...going through it to see if there was anything inside it that we could use."

"Looked to me like you were about to snort some coke."

Old habits of hiding her addiction kick in. "I was not! I was just looking through..."

Shaun yanks the bag from her hands. "You seem to forget I'm a cop. Or I was one. Not sure what I am now."

Her shoulders sag as she continues limping down the path back toward the cave. "Join the club, dude. I was thinking the same thing while running earlier. We probably all are."

"Stop. We need to talk."

"Ain't got nothing to discuss."

Flinching at Shaun's touch, she stops.

He spins her around. "I know what I saw, and what you were about to do. I also know about your past struggles with narcotics. Everyone in town did. Do you have any idea how much pain you caused your mom? Did she ever tell you she almost died right after you ran off?"

"What're you talking about? And how the fuck would you know?"

"Because I was there the night a bullet missed her by inches. I came in as backup on a domestic call. She wasn't thinking about what she was doing because she was worried about you. She never saw the gun the perp had, but I did. I saved her that night, and she saved me yesterday. Don't add another stain to her memory."

She swallows hard, forcing her tears back down. "I never knew that. Could've lived the rest of my life without knowing, either."

"You needed to hear it. Use it as strength to stay clean. You know, I get why you want to take something that will make the pain go away. Believe me, I'm right there with you. But we aren't in a world that allows us the luxury of escaping from reality. Not even for one minute."

Shame at almost slipping twice in forty-eight hours makes her cheeks burn. The tears come, hard and fast.

If anyone could understand the depth of sorrow inside her heart, it is Shaun Kilpatrick. "I'm so sorry about your wife...and baby...thank you for saving Mom that night."

The big man's face crumples. Tears form and he drops the satchel and turns away. "I...we...said some nasty things to each other recently, me and Marian. I didn't know the baby was mine until recently."

Unsure what to say, she moves closer and rests her hand on Shaun's trembling shoulders. "Doesn't change what happened in the store."

"No, it doesn't. I thought the mess out at deer camp was bad enough. This was...way worse. I can't deal with it, and I'm a grown man. A tough cop. Can't imagine how you must feel, which is why I understand you wanting to burn the images out of your head with drugs. Now, I finally understand how Craig felt."

"Who's Craig?"

Shaun sniffs and wipes his hand across his face. "A friend of mine. One who struggled with an addiction to cocaine after his wife died."

"Do you mean Craig Jackson?"

Turning back around to face her, he nods. "Yeah. You know him?"

"No. But my...mom did. She worked his wife's accident on I-30. When she came home after notifying him his wife had passed, it was the first time I'd seen my mom take a drink in years."

"Yeah, it was a rough scene. Traffic accidents between a car and a semi are always gruesome."

Silence falls between them, both lost in memories of a world no longer existing. Instead of talking, they stare at the sunrise. For five minutes, they watch the vibrant colors spread across the sky.

"When I was running earlier, I was pissed for a lot of reasons, but the biggest one is because I wouldn't be able to bury my mother."

"I hear you. That's one of the reasons I got up and came outside. Well, actually, I was following you like I said, but wishing I could have a service for Marian and our child was something I pondered while walking."

"What were you gonna name her? Marian never said."

Shaun clears his throat. "April. April Dawn Kilpatrick."

"That's lovely. So, how about we have our own memorial service, right here, just the two of us?"

"Great idea." Shaun smiles. "I agree with what your mom said earlier. It's your heart that will keep you going."

Jesse ignores him and bends down to gather some sticks and rocks. She forms a makeshift cross from the wood while Shaun makes two circles with the rocks. She hands one cross to Shaun and in tandem, they place them in the center of each circle.

"Would you like to say something?" Jesse whispers.

"I can't. I'm a big baby. You go ahead."

"Lord, we don't know what's going on, why, or how we're supposed to deal with all this. What we do know is our loved ones aren't here, and we miss them like crazy. Please, if you're there, take care of them. Mom…I love you so much. You were my world, and I miss you so much it hurts. Thank you seems pathetic to say how much I appreciate and respect what you did for me. For Shaun. For Marian and April. Until we meet again, Amen."

"Who the hell are you and what are you doing here?"

Jesse and Shaun both jump at the sound of an unfamiliar male voice behind them. Shaun wraps a thick arm around her back in a protective embrace.

"Put your hands up. Right now. I won't ask twice."

"Do what he says Jesse." Shaun whispers.

Leaves crunch behind them. Her anger flares, pissed at being interrupted during her last goodbyes to her mother. "I'm Jesse Parker and this is Officer Shaun Kilpatrick. What we're doing here is saying our final goodbyes to my mom and his wife. Who the fuck are you?"

"My, but aren't you a spitfire? Got any weapons?"

"If I did, I'da already put one in you. Let me guess: You're another piece of shit military man. You guys don't give up!" Jesse hisses.

"One in my holster." Shaun offers.

The man groans then moves in front of them after yanking out the pistol from Shaun's hip. Jesse's stomach tightens at the sight of him. He is big, full of rippling muscles, body covered in dirty fatigues stained with what she assumes is blood. *Another military man. I knew it!*

"How'd you end up here, in the middle of nowhere?"

"As the young woman mentioned, we're saying out last goodbyes to our loved ones." Shaun answers. "Ones who died saving our lives."

The man lowers his rifles and sighs. He hands the pistol back to Shaun. "That seems to be a problem all of us are facing nowadays. You look rough. You weren't running from him, were you?"

Jesse shakes her head. "No, of course not. We gave you our names. What's yours?"

"Kevin Warton."

"Well, Mr. Warton, are you gonna kill us just like the others planned on?"

"Others?"

Jesse lowers her arms, sensing the man no longer poses a threat. "Yeah, others. The men and women sent by the government who hunted us down, determined to carry out their orders to terminate all those who haven't been tested."

Kevin backs up and motions for them to stand. "I'm ex-military and take no orders from anyone, so no. God almighty, I can't handle any more death. Only thing I killed recently was already dead."

"Fair enough. So, what are *you* doing out here?" Shaun asks. "Didn't you hear us praying for lost loved ones? Kind of rude to just storm over."

"Trying to survive like you two are and decided to seek refuge in an area with few people. I was walking off some stress because I had to kill my best friend earlier. That's his bag you're holding. Do you mind?"

"Oh, sorry." Shaun hands the satchel back. "We didn't know."

"I...uh, tripped over it earlier. Spilled some of the stuff inside." Jesse mumbles, covering all bases in case the man is aware of the drugs.

Kevin's demeanor shifts in a flash. He furrows his brow, backs up several steps, and raises the rifle. "Spilled or snorted? Don't lie to me."

"Spilled, I swear, though I was gonna snort it up before he stopped me." Jesse motions toward Shaun. "I lost my mom yesterday and thought I'd just, you know, slip away for a bit. But I didn't take any, I promise. If you don't believe me, go look over there. You'll see. Geez, calm down. In your former life, you musta been DEA or something. Old habits die hard, right?"

Kevin lowers the rifle and steps closer, examining her face. For some reason, it reminds her of the times she'd been pulled over and given sobriety tests by law enforcement.

At least this time she'll pass. "See? My eyes aren't dilated, and I can cross them. Satisfied?"

"Guess it's your lucky day." Kevin backs away and walks down the path in the opposite direction. "Stay safe. And don't do drugs."

"Nice meeting you." Jesse's tone drips with heavy sarcasm.

"Are you trying to get us shot?" Shaun whispers.

"The dude's on serious edge. Worse than me. Just trying to lighten the mood. Mom always said I had a smart mouth."

"Better learn to censor it a bit better. Like you said, people are on edge. The longer this goes on, the edgier they'll become."

"Hey, people who use humor in stressful situations tend to live longer. Knocks others off balance."

Not ten seconds passes before Kevin yells from behind them. "Wait! I've got some questions I need to ask."

Kevin jogs across the trail until catching up. "You mentioned orders were given to terminate all those untested? What did you mean? Where are you from?"

Jesse sighs. "Malvern. A group of soldiers came in and took over the town. Tried to round up all the residents for testing. They did test some but then decided the better option was killing us all. We escaped and came here."

Kevin lets out a low whistle. "Glad Uncle Sam isn't my employer any longer. Malvern? That's a long haul through some big towns. What's it like out there?"

Jesse locks gazes with him. "You sure you want to know?"

"Nah, just making polite conversation."

"Not necessary. Social conventions are no longer needed. Now, if you don't mind, we'll be on our way."

"You got a camp close by? Any others with you?"

Jesse continues walking, trying to keep the fear from her voice. "We aren't alone, if that's what you mean. Our people will be worried if we don't show up soon, so have a nice day, Kevin."

"Seriously? That's your response? Have a nice day? Uh, nice days are over after all the dead started walking around."

Shaun pushes Jesse behind him and rests his hand on the butt of his gun. "If you don't want to join them, then leave us be. We mean you no harm, so just let us go. We'll all pretend this conversation never happened. Chalk it up to a rough last forty-eight hours."

"You'll be changing that tune when you're hungry and thirsty." Kevin snorts. "By then, I'll be long gone."

"We'll take our chances, thanks." Shaun's voice is stern.

Kevin shrugs his shoulders and walks away after slinging the pack over his shoulder. Shaun and Jesse exchange worried glances.

"Can you walk any faster?" Shaun asks.

"I'll try." She takes two tentative strides before pulling up. "I'm afraid my back and hips won't let me."

"Then I'll just carry you. You can't be any heavier than a buck."

Before Jesse can say a word, Shaun picks her up and places her over his shoulder. He takes off at a light jog, heading back toward to the cave.

"Wait…he's gone. Put me down. This is killing my back."

"You sure?"

"Yes. It's okay. Mom said I was tough, and I guess it's time to prove her right."

In silence, they trudge back through the bright woods. Jesse glances up once into the morning sky, wishing the lovely dawn is the beginning of a beautiful, new day.

It's a new day, alright, but what horrors will the light illuminate?

***

Walt lowers the rifle, nerves on edge, heart racing. He had the man who said his name was Kevin Warton in the crosshairs during the entire, strange conversation with Shaun and Jesse yet a faint niggling inside his mind warned him not to take the shot. Holding his breath, body frozen in place, he watches Jesse and Shaun head back toward the cave.

When he woke up earlier and saw Shaun go outside, he almost turned over and went back to sleep, but then he scanned the room and noticed Jesse was gone, too, so he'd follow them both in case they needed protection.

Assuming they both needed some air to clear their heads after watching their loved ones die, he followed without giving his presence away, giving them enough room to let out private tears.

When Jesse took off running, he realized she thought she was alone. His original plan was to cut back and circle in front of her before she hurt herself or ran into trouble. The stupid, former junkie was outside with nothing on but a tattered coat and unarmed. Unwilling to announce his presence, fearing there might be a hungry corpse lurking in the shadows, he remained quiet while darting through the forest.

Shaun beat him to Jesse, so he crouched in the shadows and watched their interactions, keeping an eye out while the duo consoled each other for their recent losses.

Anger rumbled around inside his chest while watching because even from a distance, he sensed a bond forming between them. Part of him understood—realized it stems from their mutual losses—another part worried where the connection might lead. Anger turned to fury when Jesse slipped back into her old habit—or almost did—had Shaun not stopped her from snorting shit up her nose.

Once a junkie, always a junkie. Jesse Parker is a liability. Unstable.

When Kevin Warton appeared, a strange mixture of fear and satisfaction competed for control of his thoughts. Fear at the realization they aren't alone, just as he suspected, and the satisfaction his gut instincts about the bag belonging to a government goon was on target.

The things Warton said made the hairs on Walt's arm stand erect. Even in the dim light, he can tell the type of man Kevin Warton was—military for sure, though he lied when questioned about it. He made up his mind to keep quiet and follow the man even before he flipped his lid when the mention of drugs came up.

What're is he doing up here? He doubts it was just him and his friend, so who else is he with, and why?

He remains still until Jesse and Shaun pass by his position, waiting until they are two-hundred yards ahead. Slipping out of the shadow of the trees, careful to keep his steps quiet, he stalks Kevin Warton as though the man is a trophy buck while mentally berating him:

My mountain. My family. You need to leave but not before I find out why you're here. I killed my friend without batting an eye, so a stranger will be a piece of cake.

The man he tried to bury—the old soldier who killed many people during deployments overseas—is beginning to take control of his mind. The first appearance happened on the rooftop when he shot Curt.

While watching and listening to the junkie whore—the one his son is in lust with—his guts burned. Though he'd changed his mind about Regina, learned to respect her for her loyalty and sacrifice to save others, he felt no warm, fuzzy feelings toward Parker's kid.

At all.

I'll protect my family at all costs. Jesse Parker isn't family, and if she stands in the way of our safety, I won't hesitate to take her down.

Mind ablaze with dark thoughts, he pulls out a hunting knife and continues following Kevin Warton, determined to find out the man's secrets.

And if he is alone.

ABOUT THE AUTHOR

Award-winning and International bestselling author Ashley Fontainne's works can be found in ebook, print, and audio.

Visit http://www.ashleyfontainne.net for more information.

SNEAK PEEK AT TAINTED FUTURE

Chapter 1 - Waking up in Hell
Monday, December 22nd – 5:15 a.m. – Mountain Standard Time

COOPER HOLLINGSWORTH stares at the bloody snow. The crimson patches make the thick, white powder look like someone tossed buckets of red juice all over the ground. He is surrounded by slushies made from human blood. Mind reeling, he barely notices the lone streetlight flickering, bouncing flashes of light across the area. To him, it feels like watching a horror movie and any second, eerie music will fill the parking lot of the gas station.

He wishes someone would yell "end scene" and the nightmare would be over.

That isn't going to happen.

The knowledge this is all real makes him puke. Bending over, he vomits until nothing is left to expel from his body except saliva.

The gun in his hand feels like it weighs thirty pounds, but he won't put it back inside the holster. It is too risky. More of them may be lurking about, drawn to the sound of the shots he fired only minutes ago.

Eight spent shell casings rest in small divots in the snow next to his feet. The wind picks up speed, stirring the top layer of fresh powder into a whirling vortex of white. The sharp, cold shards pepper his exposed face, making his eyes water. The wind isn't the only reason tears streak down his cheeks and chin.

"This isn't real. It can't be." He whispers to the dead corpses on the ground. "God, Karla. I'm so sorry."

Fear reaches inside his chest and latches its cold, strong tentacles around his heart. Pausing to listen for signs of any others, his fingers twitch with nervous anticipation. Hearing nothing, he blows out a huff of air, watching the vapors linger above him before disappearing into the darkness.

The earlier, continual sounds of explosions, gunfire, and people screaming had faded into sporadic bouts of noise after leaving Steamboat Springs. For hours, he and Karla wound their way through the treacherous, twisty roads leading out of Steamboat toward Denver. Karla had been in a state of shock, alternating between crying and yelling while he dodged stalled vehicles and mangled corpses.

The carnage surrounding him fades out. Disturbing memories of how they ended up on the run for their lives fill his vision. He leans against the cold hood of the SUV and weeps.

***

"Cooper? Honey, wake up. Something's wrong."

Every muscle in his body aches from a long afternoon the day before hiking through the snow-covered trails. Even though Karla had a map, they still managed to get turned around and ended up wandering for hours. By the time they arrived back at their vehicle, both were cold and exhausted.

Groaning, he rolls over and snuggles closer to his wife's warm body. He opens one eye and scans the dark room, guessing it is close to dawn.

"Go back to sleep, baby. We're in the mountains. It's probably a moose or deer foraging around outside. Maybe even a cougar out hunting for breakfast."

Karla's grip intensifies on his arm; slender fingers dig into the flesh. "I know what animals sound like, Cooper Hollingsworth. They don't scream like humans!"

The terror in his wife's voice forces him to open both eyes. Pulling Karla closer, assuming she is freaked out from a nightmare, he tries to offer comfort, but his doubts about what she heard vanish the second several shrill, ear-piercing screams fill the dark bedroom. The wails send chills up his spine. He recognizes the abject fear in the voices.

Fully awake, he reverts to cop mode, motioning for Karla to remain quiet while he eases out from under the covers. Padding across the cold hardwood, he reaches the bookcase where his cell and gun sit. Snatching up his pistol, he peers out the window while simultaneously dialing 9-1-1.

"We're sorry, all circuits are busy. Please try your call again later."

He hears the words in his ear from the robotic voice, yet they really don't register because his attention is on three women running through the parking lot. The new layer of snow and ice on the pavement makes their attempts to flee a wasted effort. They slip and slide across the ground. One of them falls, and the remaining two scramble to pick her up.

The parking lot lights of the rental condos provide enough light for him to see every detail. He recognizes the girls from their long, bright red hair—the triplets named Margo, Margie, and Marie. They'd bumped into each other while unpacking their vehicles the day before.

The three young women were celebrating their twenty-first birthdays in the awe-inspiring mountains of Steamboat Springs. The girls are beautiful, full of energy and spunk, and only a few inches shy of his 6'1" frame. Even though he is celebrating his anniversary with his lovely bride, he couldn't help but admire their curves and sexy smiles while they carted overstuffed suitcases from their vehicle.

Margo mentioned in passing their boyfriends surprised them with the combined Christmas and birthday present of a week in the mountains. Margie had laughed and said the surprise was really on their men because they'd missed their flight from Boise and would have to drive in. Marie giggled while holding a box full of liquor, commenting about how the boys would miss out on ravishing their drunk girlfriends the first night.

Are the men chasing the girls their boyfriends or just locals who decided to take advantage of three women alone?

Stepping away from the window, he looks around for his clothes.

"What's going on, honey? Did you see anyone?" Karla whispers while turning on the bedside lamp.

"Looks like a major falling out between the triplets and their dates. Stay here and keep trying to call 9-1-1." He yanks on a pair of jeans and a coat before sliding on his slippers. "I'm going to help those girls. Seems like the boyfriends—"

"No! Oh, my God! Margo! Margie! Somebody help us!"

Double-checking the magazine to make sure it is full; he glances over at Karla. Her big, green eyes are the size of saucers.

Darting out of the bed, she makes a beeline for her cell phone. "Quit talking and get! I'm on it."

"Give them code 10-17 and advise out-of-state law enforcement is on scene and armed. I don't want them shooting me."

Karla nods while putting her robe on. Turning, he races down the stairs, opens the front door, and is immediately slapped in the face by the cold mountain air. How the girls are outside without coats on—and the men only in their underwear—he cannot fathom. Based on the impact to his skin, the temperature hovers near zero.

Forcing himself to take even, calculated steps on the treacherous walkway, he makes it out to the parking lot. The first orange and yellow rays of the sun peek over Mount Werner, but have yet to touch the valley, forcing him to rely on instincts while navigating in the dark. In the distance, the faint sound of yelling and the distinct *pop pop pop* of gunfire make his skin prickle.

What the Hell is going on?

The screaming stops and he knows this isn't a good sign. His heart pounds in his ears, adrenaline in overdrive as he rounds the corner of the building, rather surprised none of the other vacationers are outside trying to help. He brushes the thought away, remembering he isn't in a small, southern town in Arkansas. This is Colorado, and though Steamboat isn't a huge town, it is bigger than Malvern. Obviously, the big city mentality of "mind your own business" reigns supreme.

The bright lights cast from several security lamps in the parking lot guide the way and allow him a full visual of what is happening to Marie, Margo, and Margie. All three girls are down, their fire-engine red hair in stark contrast against the white snow. Two of the men appear to be fighting with each other over one, and the remaining male has his head down on…

"No way!"

His brain tries to comprehend the improbable scene. Raising the pistol, he stops about twenty yards away and plants his feet.

"Police! Hands up and get away from them right now or I'll shoot. This is your only warning."

The man closest to him, the one with his face buried in the stomach of one of the triplets, raises his head and turns toward the sound of Cooper's voice. A sick feeling spreads throughout his chest.

The movement is nothing near the fluid motions of a person and reminds him of several horror movies he'd watched with his kids—the kind filmed in a jumbled mash of shots where the monster lurches and shudders with unnatural, inhuman steps.

Acid burns in his stomach when he realizes the man's face is covered in blood. The wind shifts and the rank stench of bowels make him gag. Entrails hang from the man's mouth; tendrils of steam from warm flesh surround his head. The man continues chewing while his hand shovels more intestines into an already full mouth.

The girl is dead. No one could remain quiet while being eviscerated or survive with an empty body cavity.

Without hesitating, he fires. The bullet tears through the man's chest, center mass, yet doesn't faze him in the least. The impact knocks him to the ground, but before Cooper can blink twice, the man is on his feet, making short order of the distance between them.

Motion to the right catches his attention. The other two men stopped fighting, drawn to the sound of the gunshot. Stunned and in shock the bullet hadn't killed the first man, he shuts out the crazy thoughts spinning through his mind. He pushes away the law-abiding cop, the one trained to diffuse a volatile situation with minimal force; brushes off what the aftermath might be when the incident makes the news. It will be the kind filled with headlines about a rogue cop losing control and blowing holes in innocent civilians.

He doesn't care because something is very, very wrong with these men. Alarm bells ring inside his mind, warning him if he doesn't take out the three bastards, they'll continue killing until someone else intervenes.

While exhaling, he steadies his aim and fires again. The round pierces the space between the man's eyes, blowing chunks of brain matter, skull, and gore as it exits the back. The body collapses in midstride with a loud *thump*.

Turning his focus on the other two, who are less than ten feet away, he doesn't hesitate. In less than two seconds, he takes in every visual, auditory, and sensory input. The boys—*no, things*—are directly under the light in the parking lot. There is a weird, bluish array of zigzagging lines all over their bodies. The coppery odor of blood fills the air.

A shudder of fear wracks his body. There are no puffs of air streaming from their mouths; no rise and fall of their chests.

They aren't breathing.

Both sets of hands are covered in red. Blood dribbles down their chins and onto bare chests. One opens his mouth and hisses, almost like a pissed off cat. Each has the same awkward gait as the other. Their eyes are solid black.

Acid? PCP? Something new? What kind of drug turns eyes black as coal and stops a person from breathing, yet allows them to keep moving? Even the sclera is dark! Like that matters, dumbass. They. Aren't. Breathing.

"One more step and I'll—"

The grumbling, guttural roar from both men makes sweat burst from Cooper's skin. Two quick, well-placed shots later, their halting advancement is over. All three men are down, dark rivulets of thick, mahogany-colored blood seeps from their wounds into the snow. A light groan from one of the girls causes his heart to skip two beats.

Sidestepping the three dead men, he checks on the girl. The other two are dead, ripped to pieces as though a horde of wild hogs tore them apart. He swallows the burning stomach juices rumbling inside him.

He cannot tell which sister he is looking at because the girl's face is gone. How she is still alive—at least enough to moan—is beyond his comprehension.

Crouching next to her shredded and mangled body, he knows she won't last another two minutes. The amount of blood loss is staggering, and even if she was at a hospital and on an operating table, she stands no shot of surviving. Bubbles of blood ooze from the gaping wound in her neck. He can see every one of her white teeth—including the back molars—since the skin and most of the flesh on her face has been torn off. Rather than let her die in the cold snow alone, he reaches out, takes her frozen hand in his, and squeezes.

www.ingramcontent.com/pod-product-compliance
Lightning Source LLC
Chambersburg PA
CBHW050040180626
46810CB00002B/818